P9-BYB-476

The bus door opened, and a swarthy ma[n] [in a] jacket climbed aboard. The door cl[osed] behind him, and the bus started up agai[n.] glanced about the interior of the bus and [asked the] driver, "Is this all of them? I thought we fig[ured at] least eight."

The bus turned and started north, direc[tly away] from Valley Gardens. Dexter, who had been st[aring in] bewilderment, came to with a start.

"Hey, you can't do this! Who do you thi[nk you] are, anyway? Where do you think you're taking [us?]"

The man in the leather jacket was standing [with] his back against the door.

"I think you had better move," he said. "And [you,] girl"—he nodded to Jesse—"you move up with hi[m. I] want you all together where I can keep tabs on yo[u."]

Perched at the front of the bus, Bruce stared back at them all like a small, startled owl.

"What—what's happening?" he asked shakily. "Glenn, do you understand?"

His brother's handsome face was incredulous. H[e] drew a long breath.

"It looks," he said in a strange, flat voice, [as] though we are being kidnapped."

LOIS DUNCAN

RANSOM

LAUREL-LEAF
BOOKS

for Robin Dale

Published by
Laurel-Leaf
an imprint of
Random House Children's Books
a division of Random House, Inc.
New York

This work has been published under the title *Five Were Missing*. All the characters in this book are fictitious, and any resemblance to actual persons, living or dead, is purely coincidental.

Visit us on the Web! www.randomhouse.com/teens

Educators and librarians, for a variety of teaching tools, visit us at www.randomhouse.com/teachers

ISBN: 0-440-97292-2

RL: 5.3

Reprinted by arrangement with Doubleday Books

Printed in the United States of America

One Previous Edition
First Laurel-Leaf Edition December 1990
New Laurel-Leaf Edition June 2005

60 59 58 57 56 55 54 53 52 51

OPM

Chapter One

The kidnapping took place on a Thursday.

"If it had been Friday," Jesse said afterward, "I wouldn't have taken the bus at all. I would have stayed in the library and read until Mother picked me up after her committee meeting."

There were a lot of ifs.

"If my car had not been in the garage," said Glenn.

And Marianne Paget thought: If I had taken that ride with Rod when he offered it to me, when he drove all the way over to the high school just to pick me up.

But, she had not. She had climbed onto the bus with the others, swinging her hips a little so that her plaid skirt flared about her, holding her slim shoulders defiantly straight beneath the blue suede jacket.

I have hurt him, she thought, and the knowledge was strangely satisfying. I have hurt him, and by hurting him, I have shown Mother and all of them.

When she took her seat, she leaned forward and looked

out the window to where Rod was standing beside his car, staring in a defeated way at the door she had just entered.

What can she see in him? Marianne asked herself bitterly. He is so dull, and his hair is going—it won't be long now before he is completely bald. Imagine Mother having a bald husband! How can she like him—how can she even stand him—after living with Daddy?

The man by the car was still standing there, still watching the bus door as though half hoping that she might change her mind and get off again.

You would think he would begin to realize, thought Marianne, but no, he will go home and tell Mother, and he will be just as hurt and surprised as though it were the first time. And Mother will say, "Give it time, dear. It's just a phase. She hasn't adjusted yet. It will be all right in time." But it will be one more thing, one more wedge between the two of them. And it will not be long before they will have to know that time will make no difference. Time will not change a thing.

The bus filled quickly. From her seat near the back, Jesse French watched the other students pouring in, laughing, shoving, tossing their books about. They crowded into the double seats, and Jesse, sitting alone, felt the empty space beside her becoming more and more obvious as it was ignored by first one person and then another.

There was a moment when she thought Glenn Kirtland was going to sit there. He seemed to hesitate for an instant, and then his eyes went ahead, and he moved forward and took the seat next to Marianne.

I should have known, Jesse thought, that he wouldn't sit here—and she let herself relax again, not certain whether the sudden caved-in feeling was relief or disappointment. If he had sat next to her, she would have had to talk to

6

him, and what could one say to a boy like Glenn, the president of the student body and captain of the football team? Jesse, who could speak to adults with ease and graciousness, who could discuss art and history and politics with Frenchmen and Germans and Italians in their native tongues, found herself weak and tongue-tied at the idea of talking school and sports with Glenn Kirtland.

If he weren't so popular, she thought—but, of course, that was only an excuse, for popular people *were* popular because they were easy to talk to. There was Marianne now, chattering away to him already, turning in her seat to face him, letting her soft blond hair fall forward across her cheek. But then, Marianne was popular, too. She was pretty and pert and bubbly and had undoubtedly never had a moment's self-consciousness in her life.

"May I sit here?"

Jesse glanced up and nodded, and Bruce Kirtland took the seat that his brother had not occupied. Bruce was only a freshman, a thin boy with glasses and a nervous, overeager, puppy-dog look. He sat down too quickly, and his books tumbled across his knees, and a pencil case slid off onto the floor. Bruce stooped for it, and the books fell also.

"I'm sorry. Gosh, there goes another!"

"Here, let me hold those others. You're going to lose them, too."

Jesse reached over and steadied the remaining two books, wondering, as she did so, how someone like Glenn could possibly have a brother as awkward as Bruce. At the same time she felt a wave of sympathy for this boy, who would have to live, always, in the shadow of Glenn.

"Do you have them?" she asked kindly as he bobbed up from the floor, his face flushed with exertion.

"Yes, I think so. Gee, I'm sorry."

7

"That's all right." She had her own books piled neatly on her lap—math, which she detested, and chemistry, and a French novel which she was reading for pleasure. Normally she would have opened it the moment she was settled, but now, because it was Bruce next to her and because he was so obviously embarrassed about his clumsiness, she felt duty-bound to make at least a few minutes of conversation.

"It's really turning cold," she said.

"Yes, it is." Bruce leaned across her to gaze out the window. "It looks kind of like snow, doesn't it? It's coming late this year." His voice was hopeful. "If Glenn gets his car out of the shop this afternoon, we may be able to go up to Taos."

"To ski?" Jesse asked politely. "That should be fun. Do you like skiing?"

"I like it fine, but I haven't gone too many times. Glenn's usually got a bunch of his friends going. Boy, he's good—my brother! You ought to see him come down Snake Dance!"

He sat back in his seat, and Jesse, nodding, realized that her sympathy had been misplaced. There was no jealousy here, only a glow of pride in his brother's accomplishments.

"Glenn can even take jumps. You know the ski pro at Taos? He says Glenn is one of the best skiers who come up there." He paused and then added politely, "Do you ski?" and Jesse answered, "I haven't skied here in New Mexico. We've been here only since summer."

"You'll learn," Bruce told her consolingly. "There are lots of beginners," and Jesse, who had been about to add the fact that the last time she had skied it had been in the Swiss Alps, left the words unspoken and smiled at him instead.

"I'm sure I'll like it," she said.

Dexter Barton was the last one to get on the bus. His sixth period was gym class, and it always made him late because he didn't like using the community showers. He hung around the gym, bouncing balls and putting away the exercise mats until the first rush was over, and then went into the dressing room just as most of the other fellows were leaving. If he was lucky and the shower was empty, he used it; otherwise he yanked his clothes on as quickly as possible, trusting to the general rush and confusion of late dressing to cover the omission of bathing. By the time he was clothed and had put away his gym clothes, it was a matter of luck whether or not he was able to make the bus before it pulled out of the lot. Sometimes he didn't, and it meant hitchhiking, something he did not particularly mind when the weather was warm.

Today, however, the wind had a nasty nip to it, and the idea of his standing for half an hour on a street corner, thumbing a ride, was a far from pleasant one. He put on a final burst of speed and jogged up to the bus just as the door was closing. He grabbed it with his good left hand and yanked it open and clambered up the steps, glancing about him for a seat. The only one left was near the back, by a window, and he had to climb over a giggly sophomore girl to reach it.

"You might at least say excuse me," she told him coyly, and her counterpart, in the seat directly across the aisle, giggled also.

"Excuse me," Dexter said.

"Think nothing of it, I'm sure." Her mock New York accent was a teasing duplication of his own, and she fluttered her eyelashes at him flirtatiously. "You wouldn't by any chance be from the East, would you?"

"Yes," Dexter said coldly, not rising to the bait. He wedged himself into the corner and turned his face to the window, not so much to see out as to avoid contact with his seatmate.

The bus had ground into motion now, moving out of the school driveway, slowly, slowly turning into the street. It lurched a little and swung wide to avoid the Drive Slowly— School Zone sign which marked the middle line, and it seemed to straighten with an effort. To Dexter, who was always conscious of mechanics, it was immediately apparent that something was not as usual. He turned his gaze from the window and straightened in his seat, trying to see to the front. Glenn Kirtland's head blocked him, and he pulled himself higher.

"What are you looking at?" asked the girl next to him.

"The driver," Dexter told her shortly.

"Is something the matter with him?"

"He's different. He's not the guy who usually drives us."

"Oh? I hadn't noticed." Now she, too, rose, leaning out into the aisle to gain a better view. "You're right, he is different. A young fellow. Say, he's cute. Look at those shoulders!"

Ignoring the comment, Dexter sank back into his seat.

"I wonder if he's going to be our regular driver from now on or if he's just a substitute." The girl looked at Dexter inquiringly. (As though, he thought, I should know the answer. As though I gave a darn whether the guy with the shoulders was going to drive every day or not.)

When she received no answer, she flushed a little and looked ahead again.

"He *is* cute," she murmured, and her friend across the aisle giggled in agreement.

"Those shoulders!"

"All that red hair—"

"A positive movie star, worth riding the old bus for."

Idiot girls, thought Dexter. The old, familiar hurt was in him, the aching, sick feeling which had been there so long now that it was almost a part of him. He should have grown used to it by this time, and yet something like this—a dumb comment from a couple of flutter-headed females—could bring it up, sharp, against his insides with a jab which was almost physical in its intensity.

"Those shoulders—"

He scowled out the window, forcing his eyes to the mountains, half hidden in clouds, to the bleak white sky, stretching on above them.

It's going to snow, he thought.

He turned his thoughts to the snow, to the cold air against his face and the feel of skis beneath his feet, to the perfect moment of freedom as he stood at the top of a run, gazing out over the long white slope that stretched before him, like a bird at that last, crucial instant before taking flight.

If I only had a car, he thought, I would take the whole weekend skiing. I'd go up to Santa Fe, maybe even to Taos. If Uncle Mark should fly to the Coast, if I could get the keys to the Jaguar—

Of course, that would not happen. It never did happen at the right times. This was when it would have been good to be a friend of Glenn Kirtland, with his Thunderbird with the ski rack on top—but no, it wouldn't be worth it. Dexter couldn't bring himself to be hypocritical enough to bootlick somebody like Kirtland just for the sake of a ski weekend.

"What's wrong with him?" the girl across the aisle

whispered, and Dexter's seatmate gave him a sideways glance and said, "Stuck-up." She deliberately said it just loudly enough to carry, but he was scowling out the window, his dark brows drawn together, his eyes on the mountains.

He did not hear her.

"Hey," one of the smaller boys near the front of the bus said suddenly. "Hey, mister, you missed our stop! That was it back there at the corner of Rosemont!"

"Sorry, kid, I guess I overshot it. I'm new on this route." The driver lowered the stop signal on the side of the bus and slowed it to a quivering halt in the middle of the block. "You'll have to walk back to it."

For the first time since the bus had left the schoolyard, general attention was centered upon the driver.

Marianne stared in surprise.

"Don't you have a list?" she asked. "Mr. Godfrey always gives his substitutes a list of the stops. Did he forget to this time?"

"He didn't have a chance," said the driver. "It was real sudden, his getting sick. They just called me in about an hour ago."

"So he is a substitute," the girl beside Dexter murmured to her friend, "and not a replacement," and the other girl sighed regretfully and said, "Just our luck! Tomorrow we'll lose this doll and go back to dear old gray-haired Mr. Godfrey."

"How about one of you kids sitting up front with me," suggested the driver, "to tell me where the stops are? Somebody who lives at the end of the route and knows where everybody else gets off?"

There was a moment's silence, and then Bruce Kirtland

said, "I will. I live at Valley Gardens. That's the last stop."

"That's fine then." The driver had opened the door by now, and the first group of students descended, stretching and grumbling about the short walk back to the bus stop. Bruce got up from his seat beside Jesse, dropping books and pencil case, and clambered his way down the aisle to the front of the bus.

The door closed again, and with a grinding of gears, the bus lurched forward.

"He doesn't seem to know much about handling a bus," Glenn remarked in a low voice, regarding the driver with curious eyes.

"He's just a substitute," Marianne reminded him. "Perhaps he hasn't had experience driving one."

"Even substitutes have to have special licenses. They pass tests. You can't pull in just anybody to substitute driving a school bus."

This would be the day, Glenn thought ruefully, that my car would be out of commission. At this rate we'll be lucky to get home in time for dinner. He regarded his brother, perched uncomfortably on the little seat next to the driver, patiently listing the stopping places on the route ahead. Good old Bruce, he thought—everybody's little helper.

He glanced sideways at Marianne and found her smiling.

"Your brother's a nice kid."

"Yeah, Bruce is all right. He's a real eager beaver." There was a note of condescension in Glenn's voice, and he corrected it quickly. "You should see him at home. The original plate-carrier-outer and picker-upper-after people. He even replaces my broken shoelaces!"

13

"If my little brothers ever did that, I'd faint." Marianne hesitated. "Of course, there was a time . . ."

"Yes?" Glenn did not like broken sentences.

"Well, Jay and Jackie used to be pretty good little fellows. We were a pretty close family once. Things were different when Daddy was there."

"I know." Glenn put the proper note of sympathy into his voice. He wished Marianne would not refer so often to her broken home. It did not make him uncomfortable; it simply bored him. So her parents were divorced. So her mother had remarried. What made that so terrible? It happened to people all the time.

"It's tough," he said softly, "life's tough sometimes," and he was rewarded by the look of gratitude in Marianne's eyes. They were lonely eyes, smoke-colored and large in the small, pert face. She had a good figure, too, small-boned and trim and at the same time curved in all the right places.

"Things will be all right," he said, "just wait and see."

"It makes me feel better," Marianne said, "just talking to you."

"I'm glad."

Watching her reaction, Glenn felt pleased with himself. It was so easy, really, to say the right thing to people. You could do it without even thinking. You just looked at them as though they were special and said whatever the thing was that you thought they would most like to hear, and nine out of ten times you scored. It was so easy that he had no patience whatsoever with people like Bruce who were so eager, so pathetically hopeful about having people like them that they always managed to bumble things.

"It's a shame I didn't have the car today," Glenn said.

"We could have made it home half an hour ago. It's been in the shop since Tuesday getting a new paint job. I feel as though my wings have been cropped."

"Rod, my stepfather, came by school for me." There was a hard note in Marianne's voice. "He said he was going home early."

"Why didn't you ride with him?" Glenn asked her.

"I—I just didn't want to."

"Well . . ." He smiled at her, the wide, open smile that crinkled his eyes and lit up his whole face. "It's kind of dirty, but if I have to take the misery of a school bus ride, I'm just as glad you're here to share it with me."

Marianne found herself smiling back, despite herself. "I'm glad, too," she said softly.

The bus stopped again, and more students got out. The load was thinning now.

Dexter Barton was relieved that he now had a seat completely to himself. He slouched sideways to take up as much room as possible, against the off chance that somebody might decide to change seats and sit there.

Across the aisle, the girl with the straight dark hair was sitting alone, too, as she had been ever since Bruce Kirtland had moved to the front of the bus. She lifted her head, and their eyes met, but neither made a gesture, and an instant later the girl picked up a book that had been lying on the seat beside her and opened it and began to read. It was very definitely an invitation not to move over and start a conversation, and Dexter was amused by it.

Another loner, he thought, and he would have liked her if she had not looked so much like another girl he had known. It was a type he was drawn to, tall and slender, not pretty exactly but smooth, with neat, shoulder-length hair which defied the current fashions, a cool, aloof, slightly superior lift of the head which made it seem as though there were more there than she would ever see fit to offer anybody.

The girl back in New York a couple of years ago had had that same long-lined, fine-boned look to her, the same proud, little tilt of the head. He had dated her a few times. He might have kept on dating her if it had not been summer and if the crowd had not decided to go to Coney Island.

He had made an excuse not to go, and they all had accepted it. It would have been all right if he had not overheard the girl—his girl—saying to a friend, "Thank goodness Dexter isn't going to go with us. He's a nice guy and all that, and cute enough in a jacket, but I think I'd die if I ever had to be seen on the beach with him!"

The bus stopped, started, stopped. More students got out. Now there were only five of them left, five and the driver.

We're almost there, thought Jesse. In a few moments they would turn south on the road that led into the Valley Gardens area, down behind the country club.

Valley Gardens, she thought, keeping her eyes on her book, not really reading, but concentrating on the neat white margins in order to keep from having to make conversation with the boy across the aisle who kept staring at her so rudely. Valley Gardens. A nice name. But living there had not accomplished the magical transformation that her mother had so hopefully anticipated.

"Valley Gardens." It had had a ringing sound when her mother said it, like a bell pealing across rolling countryside. "It's the nicest area in Albuquerque. A lovely place. A solid place, where people build homes and live in them for the rest of their lives."

16

Her father had shaken his head, uncomprehendingly. "I don't see why you don't want to live on the base the way we always do. It's much more convenient. I'll be near my work. You'll be close to the commissary. There's the officers' club . . ."

"But, Clark, Valley Gardens!" Mrs. French had regarded him pleadingly. "Imagine finding a house to rent there! The owners are going to Hawaii for the winter; they don't want to leave the place unoccupied. It's such a wonderful opportunity for Jesse!"

"For Jesse?" Colonel French had looked surprised. "Why for Jesse?"

"Because it will give her a chance to know people. It's the last chance we'll have, Clark, to live together as a family in a settled community. We've always flown about so, from one base to another, one country to another—"

Colonel French had gazed at her in bewilderment. "I thought you liked it—the service life. You've always said you liked it!"

"I do, dear," Mrs. French said softly. "I always will. It's Jesse I'm thinking of. She's grown up with such a mixed background. Half of her schooling has been at home. In some ways she is more like an adult than a teen-age girl, and in others she is more like a child. She has never had a chance at the solid, ordinary life that most youngsters take for granted. I want her to have a taste of this kind of life. I want her to make her friends among a young crowd from the good society of the town, to be part of a crowd, to come out of her shell and belong somewhere."

"Jesse?" Her father had turned to her. "Do you want this? Do you want to live in Valley Gardens?"

"I—I don't care." She really hadn't. "If Mother wants it so much, I—I think it's fine."

It would make no difference. She had known that it would not, but she could not bear to crush the glow in her mother's eyes.

"I'd like to live there, Dad."

"Women!" Her father had shaken his head helplessly. "Give them Paris in the springtime, Switzerland in the summer, and what is their prize dream? To spend a winter in Valley Gardens, New Mexico."

So they had moved into the rental house. "The only rented house," Mrs. French kept remarking, "in Valley Gardens." And Jesse had still been Jesse. It had really made no difference.

Because her eyes were on the book, she was not the one to notice first that the bus had passed the turnoff. It was Bruce's voice that brought it to her attention.

"Hey, we've come too far! Back there is where I told you to turn, back by the sign to the country club. You can pull right through the gates into the Gardens, and we all get off there."

"That's okay." The driver hardly seemed to notice him. "I'm taking the long way 'round. I have to stop and pick up a friend of mine."

"Pick somebody up? With the school bus?" Bruce was surprised.

In her own seat Marianne echoed his reaction. "That's funny. Whom would he pick up with the bus? And why? It's not as though it were public transportation or something."

"Well, we'll see in a minute. He's slowing down." Glenn leaned past her to gaze out the window with curiosity. "I guess that's the friend he's stopping for. It sure does seem peculiar."

The bus door opened, and a swarthy man in a leather jacket climbed aboard. The door closed quickly behind

18

him, and the bus started up again. The man glanced about the interior of the bus and said to the driver, "Is this all of them?"

"These are the kids from the Gardens area." The driver spoke over his shoulder, his eyes on the road ahead.

"But there are only five. I thought we figured on at least eight." The new passenger spoke with a marked Mexican accent, not unusual in this part of the country. "Only five. Geez, Buck, it's hardly worth the risk of it."

"We'll make it worth it," the driver told him.

The bus turned now and started north, directly away from Valley Gardens. Dexter, who had been staring in bewilderment, came to with a start.

"Hey, you can't do this! Who are you anyway? Where do you think you're taking us?"

The man in the leather jacket was still standing with his back against the door. Now he took a step forward.

"I think you had better move," he said, "behind those other two up there. And you, girl"—he nodded to Jesse—"you move up with him. I want you all together where I can keep tabs on you."

"What the devil . . ." Dexter began. And then he saw the pistol.

The bus turned again now, off the highway onto one of the dirt roads that led along the river.

"Where are we going?" Jesse asked numbly.

"Move forward," the man with the jacket told her, and she did so, closing her book carefully first, automatically slipping a bit of paper in to mark her place, too stunned even to attempt to grasp the significance of what was happening.

"You, too," the man said, and Dexter followed her, growling defiance beneath his breath, but moving.

Perched at the front of the bus, Bruce stared back at them all like a small, startled owl.

"What—what's happening?" he asked shakily. "Glenn, do you understand?"

His brother's handsome face was incredulous. He drew a long breath.

"It looks," he said in a strange, flat voice, "as though we are being kidnapped."

Chapter Two

Marianne Paget was often misjudged because of her appearance. Because she was a small girl and brought out protective instincts, because she was cuddly and big-eyed and appealing, it was easy for people to assume that the softness and helplessness which appeared on the surface went all the way through.

In reality, this was not the case. Beneath the soft hair and pert face, Marianne had a hard core of self-sufficiency. It was like a thin strand of steel wire running through the center of her being—a hidden, unbreakable resistance which kept her calm in emergencies and unbendably stubborn in the face of adversity.

It was Marianne, sitting quietly in her seat by the window, who was first able to accept the incredible situation for what it was.

They are going to hold us, she thought, for ransom. They have selected the five of us because we live in Valley Gardens, and the people who live there are supposed to have money. They can't know how it is with Mother, that she got the house when she divorced Daddy, but aside from that great, big, sprawling white elephant, she doesn't have anything.

She could imagine her mother receiving the ransom note, standing there, white-faced and shaken, and then undoubtedly bursting into hysterics. Her mother, so gentle and blond and pretty, looking exactly the way Marianne herself would look twenty years from now, lacked the element of strength that ran through her daughter. Whenever pressures got too great, she broke into pieces.

Poor Mother, Marianne thought worriedly, it is going to be terrible for her. She won't know what to do. How much money will they ask her for? A lot, I'm sure—thousands and thousands of dollars.

She recalled the words the bus driver—the other man had addressed him as "Buck—had spoken a few moments earlier.

"It's hardly worth the risk of it," the man with the Mexican accent had said, and Buck had answered, "We'll make it worth it."

Yes, they will ask her for a fortune, Marianne thought, and she won't have it, and Rod certainly won't, not from working for a newspaper like the *Journal*. There isn't even anybody they can borrow it from. They don't have rich friends the way Daddy did.

She paused, letting the words repeat themselves in her head. "The way Daddy did." And then, suddenly, it came. It was like a great burst of light switching itself on inside her, the wonderful, illuminating knowledge of what the final recourse would have to be. It was inevitable. There was simply no way out of it. The money would have to come from her father.

She will call him, Marianne told herself, and he will come. He will have to come because after all, I am his daughter! They will see each other again, and they both will be worried. Daddy will walk into the living room, and Mother will be there, crying.

She pictured the scene the way it would be, with her mother seated, weeping, on the sofa, small and frightened and desperately alone. Her father would pause in the doorway, his big frame almost filling it, his own face ashen with strain.

"Marian," he would say, and her mother would raise her head.

"Jack! Oh, Jack, I knew you'd come!"

"Of course, I've come. The moment I got your telegram. Did you think it possible that I wouldn't come when something has happened to our daughter, our Marianne!"

"Oh, Jack." And her mother would rise to her feet, holding out her hands beseechingly. "I've been so frightened! I haven't known what to do!"

"It's all right," big Jack Paget would say. "I'm here now. I'll take care of things. Now I'm home again, everything is going to be all right."

Somewhere, of course, Marianne had to admit to herself ruefully, Rod Donavan would have to fit into the picture. He did live in the house now, and he was her mother's husband. It wasn't probable that he would be out of town at the crucial moment when her father returned. Rod never went out of town anyway, and even if for some reason he should be called away, he would never leave her mother in a moment of crisis.

No, he would be there, but luck could put him somewhere in the background—in the den, perhaps, watching television, or downstairs in the basement rumpus room, which he had fixed over for himself into a workshop. With Mother crying in the living room? the practical side of Marianne asked reasonably—oh, come now!

Well, anyway, he couldn't, he simply couldn't intrude on the scene of reconciliation. Not when it was going to come about so dramatically.

The bus, which had been lurching along at much too fast a speed for the unpaved road, slowed now and pulled to the side, where, Marianne could see from the window, a car and a station wagon were parked in the shadow of a cottonwood. Beyond the tree was the river, shallow and sluggish, more mud than water in its winter lassitude. It was empty country, this part of the valley, a stretch of flatness leading off in all directions without a trace of civilization, not even a trickle of chimney smoke against the clear, unbroken arch of the sky.

There was a woman in the driver's seat of the station wagon. When the bus pulled to a stop, she opened the door and got out and stood there, huddled in her heavy coat, while the man named Buck pressed the handle that opened the bus door.

"Okay, kids," he said, "climb out and get into the station wagon."

There was a moment's silence during which no one moved or answered.

Then Glenn asked, "Why?"

"Why?" The driver regarded him with surprise. Evidently he had expected no resistance. "Because I say so, that's why. Come on, now. Get a move on."

"The joke's gone far enough," Glenn said casually. He did not sound at all worried. "I can't be late getting home today. I've got a car to pick up before the garage closes."

"This is not a joke," the man with the accent said

quietly. He had moved until he was standing in the aisle only a few feet behind them, and Marianne, although she did not turn to look at him, was as conscious of the pistol that he held as though the cold end of the barrel had actually touched her neck. She shuddered, and the man said, "Guns do not make jokes. You all are to get out of the bus."

"You wouldn't dare shoot us," Glenn told him. "You are using the gun to scare us. If you let us go now, we'll know you have only been kidding, that this was a . . . a . . . kind of initiation for a club or something. We'll just go home and not say anything to anybody and forget all about it."

He turned then and smiled, the easy, confident smile which had always won him any situation. Marianne, who knew that he must be gazing directly into the gun barrel, was filled with admiration.

He is giving them a chance to change their minds, she thought. He is telling them that they can still get out of this, that they have not yet passed the point of no return. If they are convinced that the risk is not worth it, perhaps they'll take this opportunity to let us go!

Straightening her shoulders, she forced herself to speak. "Even if—if . . . this was a real kidnapping, it wouldn't work. I mean, you couldn't get any money from my family. They simply don't have any."

Across the aisle the stocky black-haired boy with the sullen face gave a short sound which might have been meant for a laugh.

"You're sure not going to get any cash out of my uncle. He'll be glad to be rid of me. He's a bachelor, and the last thing he needs is a nephew living right on top of him."

"That's why it is a good thing this is just a joke,"

Glenn continued hopefully. "If it were for real, it wouldn't get anybody anything. So why don't we just laugh the whole thing off and—and . . ."

His voice faltered and petered out before the look on the man's face.

Marianne had turned to see it, and now shut her eyes. Oh, Lord, she thought. Oh, dear Lord, he is really going to shoot him.

In his seat at the front of the bus, Bruce thought the same thing. His face was dead white; his voice, a squeak of terror. "Glenn, don't—don't say anything else! He will shoot!"

"Yes, he will." The bus driver's tone left no room for doubt. "Juan has used that gun before. He will not hesitate to use it again. Now, for the last time, I will tell you to rise and leave the bus. Walk directly over to the station wagon and get into the back. The girls will sit on the seat. The boys will kneel on the floor facing toward the back. There will be no further discussion."

Bruce got to his feet, throwing his brother a look of panic.

Marianne reached over and touched Glenn's arm. "It's not going to work," she said softly. "I know what you were trying to do, and it won't work. They are not going to change their minds. We had better do what they tell us."

It could not be argued. Both the dark-haired boy across the aisle and the girl, whom Marianne could remember having seen on the bus on other days but whose name she did not recall, had risen and were moving forward to follow Bruce. With a shrug of defeat Glenn rose, too, and he and Marianne fell into step behind the others. They moved down the three steps to the ground and crossed to the station wagon.

RANSOM

"All right, get in." The driver had followed close behind them.

The woman in the coat moved up beside him and asked, "Is it going all right? I expected you before this."

"It took longer than I thought it would. I didn't know the stops for those other kids." His voice was brisk and businesslike. "Okay, get into the car. Girls first."

Because the other girl was hesitating, Marianne stepped past her and climbed in. As she did so, she thought, this is probably going to be our last chance to break away and run. But all reason told her that such a move would be fatal. Where was there to go in country that offered not a single rise for protection? Back along the road? Into the shallow river?

Glenn might try it, she thought, hoping desperately that he would not be so foolhardy.

But Glenn was climbing into the car.

He hesitated, and the driver said "Kneel," and he got to his knees, cramming his big frame into a cramped position on the narrow strip of floor. Marianne moved her legs over as far as possible to give him room.

To her surprise, she found that she was shaking.

Stop it, she told herself firmly. There is no sense in going to pieces. Everything is going to work out all right. It *has* to.

Beside her the other girl was crying. She was not being noisy about it; she was just sitting there, white-faced and silent, with tears streaming down her face.

Marianne reached over and took her hand. "Don't be scared," she whispered, thinking, as she said it, what an idiotic command it was.

They all were in the car now, crammed in like sardines. The boys particularly were in such cramped positions that

27

Marianne could not see how they were able to breathe. The driver closed the door and paused to secure it, in some way, from the outside. Then he and the woman got into the front, the woman in the driver's seat, and the man named Juan came around to the front of the car and handed the pistol in through the window.

"Let's get the names," he said, and Buck nodded.

"Okay, kids, give me your names. You, blondie, what's yours?"

He was looking at Marianne. She said, "Marianne Paget."

"Paget?" Buck was doing mental inventory. "Look, I don't want any funny stuff. I know who is supposed to be on that bus and who isn't. There isn't any Paget listed in Valley Gardens."

"My mother's name is Donavan," Marianne said shakily. "Mrs. Rodney Donavan. This is her second marriage. I still have my father's name."

"Donavan. Yes, that figures." He nodded, satisfied. "Next?"

They gave their names meekly.

"Jesse French."

"Glenn Kirtland."

"Bruce Kirtland."

The dark boy said, "I'm Dexter Barton. There isn't any Barton at Valley Gardens either. I live with my uncle Mark Crete."

"Crete. Okay." The red-haired man was still frowning. "That's five kids, but only four families. What about Joan Miller?"

There was a pause. Then Marianne answered, "Joan hasn't been in school this week. Her brother was hurt in an automobile accident when he was riding his motorscooter. Joan is at the hospital with her parents.''

"Well, how about the Lindleys?"

"Louise and Betty have Pep Club meeting on Thursdays."

"Just our luck!" Juan growled. "Of all days for three kids to be absent. Four families. All this risk, just for four."

"You'll have to ask enough to make it worth it," Buck said curtly. He glanced at his watch. "It's only four thirty. That's not bad, considering. Go ahead and play it just the way we planned. Rita and I will take care of the kids. You stay in town and handle the phoning. I'll call you in the morning and find out how it's shaping up."

"Right." The men exchanged quick nods.

"Oh." The Mexican hesitated. "Be sure you watch that kid—the big one. He may give you trouble."

On the floor by her knees Marianne felt Glenn stiffen.

"Don't worry," Buck said shortly. "Nobody is going to give me trouble. Come on, Rita. Let's get going."

The woman stepped on the starter. From the window Marianne could see Juan walking over to the other car. They were evidently going to leave the school bus just as it was, by the side of the road.

They were sure to find it here, she thought, and immediately she realized that it would not matter. Buck had worn gloves; he still had them on, brown leather driving gloves which would eliminate any chance of leaving fingerprints. What would the police be able to learn from the bus when they did locate it? Only that it was here, empty. They would know that the driver and passengers had been transferred to another car, but there would be nothing to show what kind of car it was or which way it had headed. With the bus here on the south end of town, parked beside the

Rio Grande, it might well be assumed that the car had proceeded south, perhaps en route to Mexico.

That, Marianne could see already, was not to be their destination. The woman had chosen the north fork in the dirt road and was turning toward the distant Sandia Mountains.

Four thirty. Marianne recalled the time as Buck had stated it, perhaps fifteen minutes ago. That made it now about a quarter to five. I should have been home forty minutes ago, she thought. Mother will be worrying, wondering what has happened. She'll probably be checking with some of the other mothers on our route. No, she will think I'm with Rod! This was a thought that had not previously occurred to her. He probably told her that he would be picking me up at school. She won't know that anything is the matter until he himself gets home.

She could picture Rod coming into the house, shedding his coat and hanging it carefully in the hall closet, not dropping it carelessly over the back of a chair, the way her happy-go-lucky father would have done. The boys would come surging to meet him, hurling themselves all over him. That was the thing she could not understand about her brothers. They had loved their father almost as much as she had, but how easily they had accepted Rod as a replacement! All he had had to do was to install a workshop and buy some airplane models and get some paint for Jay's bicycle, and there he was, king of the roost!

What callous, fickle things boys are, Marianne thought in disgust.

For her part, she had not been won over, would never be won over, no matter how many new sweaters and party dresses found their way into her bureau drawers and onto hangers in her closet. Never, as long as she lived, would she accept the name Donavan, as Jay and Jackie had done. She was Jack Paget's daughter and proud of the fact, and if she had to be the only Paget in a family of Donavans, she would be so.

Tonight, when Rod walked in, his welcome would not be as enthusiastic as usual. Despite the circumstances, the thought gave her a glimmer of satisfaction. Her mother would look at him and then past him and would ask, "Where is Marianne?"

"Marianne?" He would be surprised. "Isn't she at home?"

"I thought you were going to pick her up."

"I tried to, but she wouldn't ride with me. She insisted on taking the bus."

"She couldn't have, Rod. The bus would have had her home over an hour ago."

"But, Marian, I saw her get onto the bus myself. She must have come in without your seeing her and gone up to her room."

"But she always stops to speak to me when she comes in. Boys. No, Rod is not going to play with you now. Jay, listen to me, dear. Have you seen your sister this afternoon? Jackie, did Marianne get home while I was out in the kitchen?"

Yes, it will spoil his homecoming. They may even argue about it. And then more time will go by, and they will really begin to worry. Mother will anyway. I wonder how long it will be before that man Juan phones them? Will he do it right away or wait until late in the evening? Surely he won't wait too long. He will want to talk to them before they decide to call the police.

They had skirted the town now. Up ahead the mountains glowed an unearthly shade of pink in the late-afternoon light. In the front seat Buck was holding the pistol, but he seemed to have relaxed a bit, as though the main danger of discovery were over.

The woman was driving silently, with a clear knowledge of exactly where she was going.

From his position on the floor, Dexter shifted, trying to move his body into a slightly less awkward angle.

"Can't we sit up on the seat now?" he asked. "My legs are killing me."

"Stay where you are," Buck told him. "There isn't much chance of your making trouble when you are kneeling like that."

"We won't make trouble," Bruce said. "We promise."

"I'm not running any chance of it. There are three of you guys, and I don't want any kind of scuffle in the car. I might have to blow one of your heads off."

Next to him the woman caught her breath. "Buck, you didn't have to—"

"Not now, Rita. We'll talk about it later."

"But the old man, the one who is the regular driver. Did you—"

"I said, we'll discuss it later." He frowned at her. "Honey, use your brain. Why do you think I got Juan in on this? He's taking care of the rough stuff for us."

"And he'll make the calls?"

"All of them. He will be the only contact. His voice is the only one that anybody will hear. We're clear, you and I. All we have to do is nursemaid this little bunch for a while and then pocket the money."

Marianne shifted her position, trying to move her knees so as to make more room for Glenn, who was crouched on the floor in front of her. On the seat beside her, Jesse had stopped crying. She was leaning forward with her face in

32

her hands, and watching her, Marianne wondered if she was going to be sick. Bruce, crammed on the floor between the two older boys, looked young and scared. On the far side of him Dexter appeared to be the most miserable of all. His face was set in pain, and his legs were doubled under him at what looked to Marianne to be an impossible angle.

They rode in silence, and the mountains turned from pink to purple, and from purple to gray. The road curved upward, and the occasional approaching cars became fewer. They passed through a small town of a few stores and a couple of adobe houses and a small silver-colored church with a white steeple. After that the road became steeper.

At home, Marianne thought, they must really be worrying now. I wonder if Mother has phoned Daddy yet.

She clung to the thought, asking it over and over: Has she called him yet? Is she talking to him now?

She kept concentrating on their faces—her mother's, her father's—in the knowledge that soon, soon now they would have to be together. She let herself think no further. She closed her eyes and thought of her parents and would not watch the last pale light outside the car windows fading into night.

Chapter Three

It was dark when they reached the cabin. It had taken them three hours, Bruce Kirtland figured, trying to make out the hands of his watch in the dim light that came on in the car when the door was opened.

Three hours spent kneeling in the confinement of the floor space in front of the rear seat had numbed his legs until there was no feeling left in them. He had to grip the door and lean upon it when he got out, stamping his feet against the frozen ground to bring life back. He noticed that Glenn was doing the same.

Dexter was in an even worse state. He could not stand at all.

"He's pulling a bluff," the woman said, and Buck nodded.

"It's not going to get him anywhere." He had a flashlight beside him on the front seat, and now he switched it on, lighting the pathway from the car to the cabin. "Okay, everybody, Rita will go ahead of us and unlock the door.

34

I'll warn you now, there's no place to run, so you'd better not try to make a break for it. You'd be back in fifteen minutes, begging us to let you in before you froze.''

Dexter could not get out of the car. Bruce, who was next to him, could tell that he was trying, could see the tendons standing out in his neck as he strained to pull himself erect, and knew that it was no act.

"Here," he said, "let me help you."

He stooped and got Dexter's arm across his shoulders and then straightened, staggering a little under the unaccustomed weight.

"Sorry," Dexter muttered. "I can't."

"I know. It's okay."

Glenn stepped in then with support from the other side, taking half the weight on his strong shoulders. Between the two of them they half dragged, half carried the boy across the stretch of ground between the car and the house.

They were, Bruce realized, very high in the mountains. His breath was coming in gasps, and he could feel his heart thudding against his chest. The air was thin and bitterly cold, slicing like a knife through the jacket he was wearing and the flannel shirt beneath it. The ground under his feet was hard and slippery with frost.

It was very little warmer inside the cabin. Rita flicked the light switch in the wall by the door, and the unshielded bulb in the ceiling brought the interior into glaring view. Glancing quickly about, Bruce could see that it was the crudest sort of hunting lodge. A small kitchen opened directly to the left of the front doorway, and two other doors, evidently to bedrooms, opened opposite the front door. The living room was furnished with a wooden table and benches, a sagging couch, and several odd chairs. One entire wall was taken up with a fireplace.

A fire was already laid, and Rita went over and lit it. Of one accord, everyone moved toward the flames, and as the first tongues of heat reached them, Marianne let out a little sigh and stretched out her hands to the blaze.

Dexter detached his arm from Bruce's shoulders and sank down on the couch and began to rub his legs. Glenn's eyes never flickered from Buck and the pistol. Bruce turned his attention to Jesse, who had sat next to him on the bus. She was standing alone, a little apart from the others. Her face was very pale, and she looked as though she did not quite realize where she was or what had happened.

Bruce moved over to stand beside her. "Hey," he said softly, "are you okay?"

Slowly Jesse nodded. "I—I guess so."

"We're going to be all right. They aren't going to hurt us." He offered the first words of comfort he could think of.

"How do you know they're not?" Jesse asked him.

"I—I just don't see why they would."

"Why wouldn't they? What is there to stop them? Anyone who would do something like this—" She broke off the sentence, as though suddenly realizing that it was Bruce to whom she was talking. Her voice softened. "You're right. They won't do anything to us. They'll just ask our parents for money and let us go."

But it was too late. The doubt in her voice had infected him. He shivered suddenly, chilled inside as well as out.

Jesse saw this, and now it was she, with the responsibility of her three added years of maturity, who was the comforter. "Don't worry, Bruce; it will be all right. We'll all be home soon—just wait and see."

He was glad that Glenn was not watching him, Glenn,

who was never afraid of anything. I'm scared, thought Bruce. Oh, my gosh, I'm scared. I want to go home.

For one dreadful instant he thought he had spoken the words aloud. Then, as quickly as it had struck, the wave of panic subsided, leaving him weak and drained. I mustn't disgrace Glenn, he thought determinedly. Whatever I do, I mustn't make him ashamed of me.

The cabin was heating slowly. It was stocked with supplies, for Rita had gone into the kitchen and was opening cabinets and taking down cans. Like a picnic, Bruce thought ironically. He wished Glenn would come over and speak to him.

In his fifteen years Bruce had never once resented the fact that he was Glenn's younger brother. It was something that other people found hard to understand. Jesse's reaction had been a typical one—How difficult it must be to live always in the shadow of someone like Glenn Kirtland! Yet to Bruce, it had never seemed anything other than a privilege.

From the time he had first learned to walk, he had tottered in Glenn's footsteps. He had bypassed the usual first words of "Dada" and "Mama." It had been "Glenn"— not even a babyfied version but the full, solid name— that had been the first word he uttered.

"One nice thing about Bruce," his mother sometimes commented, "is that he doesn't have a jealous bone in his body. He adores his brother. Of course," she could not keep the note of pride from her voice, "he has good reason to."

"Glenn is going to be somebody someday," Mr. Kirtland would assert firmly.

"Not someday," Mrs. Kirtland would add softly. "Glenn is somebody already."

To Bruce, Glenn, with his looks and strength, his athletic ability, and charm and personality, had seemed to walk like a king, head and shoulders above other people's brothers. They had shared a room when they were little, before the Kirtlands had purchased their home in Valley Gardens, and Bruce, who was a light sleeper, would wake in the night and listen for the sound of Glenn's breathing. Glenn slept hard; nothing ever woke him. Lying in the darkness, Bruce would fit his own breathing to his brother's, making his chest rise and fall in the same even rhythm, feeling a closeness, a sense of intimacy, which he was never able to achieve during the daylight hours.

During the day the three-year age gap which separated the boys prevented their sharing many activities. Glenn had his set of friends, his clubs and athletics, his school and social life, which were in a realm far beyond Bruce's. Even the odd times they did spend together, there seemed to be a wall between them, an invisible barrier which Bruce could not penetrate.

It was not, he told himself firmly, a thing that was Glenn's doing. Glenn was not to blame. Glenn was nice to him, but then, Glenn was nice to everybody; it was one of his endearing qualities.

Whatever lack of closeness there was between the brothers was due, Bruce was certain, to his own inferiority. He had so little to offer in comparison with Glenn's wealth of assets. Their relationship was bound to be a lopsided one, with one brother bathed in radiance and the other merely mortal, and pretty dull mortal at that. To make up the difference, he tried to make himself useful to Glenn, keeping his things straight, hanging up his clothes when he was too busy to do so, making excuses for him when he was late or careless or forgot things.

Like the thing that had happened last Monday night.

Bruce had been in his bedroom, studying. His parents had gone to a concert, one of the symphonies of which his mother was so fond, and Glenn had been at a meeting. It had been a little after eleven when the Thunderbird pulled into the driveway. Bruce had recognized it at once by the sound of the engine and had laid his books aside and waited for Glenn to come into the house. When five minutes elapsed without this happening, he had got up and gone outside to see what was the matter.

Glenn was standing in the driveway, holding a flashlight, examining a dent in the front fender. There was a scrape as well, running along the side of the car as far as the door.

"Glenn?"

"What the devil do you think you're doing, sneaking up behind me like that!"

Bruce was not prepared for his brother's startled reaction.

"I wasn't sneaking. I just came out to see what was holding you up so long." He moved in for a closer look at the fender. "What happened?"

"I got swiped by a car," Glenn said grimly. "He came out of a side street and went right through a stop sign. I never even saw him until he hit me."

"Gee!" Bruce reached out and ran his finger along the scrape mark. "You're lucky it wasn't any worse. You'd better call in and report it—that is, if you want your insurance to cover it."

"It won't," Glenn said shortly.

"Why not? If the other guy was covered."

"He never stopped," Glenn said. "He just swung past and kept going. I didn't even get his license number. Besides . . ." He paused.

"What?" Bruce regarded him with curiosity. "Besides what?"

"I let the policy lapse."

"You let it lapse!" Bruce stared at him incredulously. "Good gosh, Glenn, how did you come to do that? Dad will hit the ceiling!"

"He won't have to know about it, I hope." Glenn was frowning thoughtfully. "I've got the cash I was saving toward new skis. I can use that to get the repairs done, and then pick up the policy again next month."

"But don't you have to report accidents?" Bruce asked. "Won't they have to know, at the garage, that it was reported?"

"I won't say it was a two-car accident. I'll just say that I scraped against a fence post or something." Glenn stood quietly, thinking through the details. "If I park the car over to the side of the driveway, Dad won't notice the fender when he comes in tonight. Tomorrow morning I'll get it into the shop. He won't even have to know."

"He'll know the car is missing," said Bruce.

"I'll tell him I'm getting a new paint job. He won't question that." He paused. "Say, Brucie?" He flicked off the flashlight.

"Yes?" Bruce strained to see his face in the sudden darkness.

Glenn's voice was strange, as though it belonged to somebody else. "You won't say anything, will you? I mean, about tonight, about the accident. If they ask you where the car is, you'll say it's being painted?"

"There's no reason they should ask me," Bruce said slowly.

"They probably won't. But there's always the chance. I mean, you will keep your mouth closed about this, won't you? If Dad found out about the lapsed policy, he'd **have** fits. He'd put me on probation for months. He might even take the car away!''

"I don't want to lie," Bruce told him. "I—I don't like having you lie either."

"Bruce, for gosh sakes, who in the world is it going to hurt? I've learned my lesson. I'll never let the insurance go again, you can be darned sure of that. What's going to be accomplished by Dad's knowing, except a lot of unpleasantness?'' There was a note of pleading in his voice. "Isn't that what brothers are for? To help each other? I'd back you up if it were the other way around."

"Well . . .''

It was so unlike Glenn's usual way of speaking, Glenn, who was always so self-sufficient.

"Come on, kid. Be a sport?''

The night was cold, and Bruce was not wearing a jacket. He shivered and hugged himself in the darkness. "Well, okay.''

"Thanks. You're a good guy." Glenn put his hand on his shoulder. It felt good there, friendly and comradely. The warmth of it went through the thin material of his shirt and filled Bruce with a sudden feeling of happiness, the same kind of closeness he had felt as a child, breathing with Glenn in the night.

"That's all right," he said.

"You're a good guy," Glenn said again, and kept his hand on his shoulder, walking beside him as they went into the house.

Now, in the cold of the cabin, Bruce wished he could bring that feeling back again. Glenn was here; they were in this thing together. The knowledge was a comfort, yet it would have been better, so much better, if Glenn had come over and stood beside him.

The cans Rita had opened contained stew, and when it was hot, she served it on paper plates at the long table. She and Buck took their own plates to the kitchen, where they could be seen through the open door, eating and talking together in low voices.

"I wonder," Marianne said softly, "what they are saying."

"They're probably discussing the ransom," Glenn hazarded. "How much money do you suppose they will ask for us?"

"As much as the traffic will bear," said Dexter. "They'll ask one amount, and then, if it looks as though that will be paid without argument, they'll up it. If I know my uncle, he'll tell them to go to blazes. I bet he doesn't come through with one penny."

"My mother won't know what to do." Jesse had not touched her food. She sat staring at the plate in front of her, as though unaware of its existence. "We don't have that kind of money. We're a service family. We don't belong in a place like Valley Gardens."

"People can get money if they have to," Marianne said comfortingly. "My parents don't live together, but I'm sure Mother will call Daddy, and he will come through somehow, even if he has to borrow. After all, we're their children."

"But Mother won't be able to get hold of my father," Jesse said. "He's off somewhere on temporary duty. We don't even know when he'll be back."

"Our parents will pay." Bruce uttered the words in a kind of desperation. "They can sell stocks and things. They will, won't they, Glenn?"

"Of course," Glenn said. For the first time he seemed to focus his full attention upon his brother and see the need for reassurance. "Don't get all shook up, Brucie. We'll get out of here."

"But when?" Bruce asked shakily. "How long will they keep us?"

Dexter was the one who answered. "As short a time as possible. Keeping us is a risk. They'll want to get rid of us as soon as they can and pocket the money and take off." He turned to Jesse, who was seated beside him, and his voice grew gentler. "Aren't you going to eat?"

She shook her head. "I'm not hungry."

"You'd better eat anyway. You need something in you."

"I can't," Jesse said weakly. She reached out and shoved the plate away and covered her face with her hands.

Bruce thought, She is going to cry again. He had watched her crying in the car on the way up the mountain, and he did not think he could bear to watch it now.

"Don't," he said. "Please."

His own control was balanced on a fine edge. He picked up his fork, concentrating on keeping it steady. He thought, I will not make Glenn ashamed of me.

Buck, who had been watching them through the kitchen door, got up and came into the living room. He stood for a moment, looking down at the group at the table, and then asked, "How is everybody doing?" His voice was pleasant, even friendly, as though he were the host at a party.

When no one answered, he said, "We're not running a restaurant here, you know. Our supplies are limited. If I were you, I'd go ahead and eat."

Marianne raised her head and met his eyes defiantly. "What are you going to do with us?" she asked. "How

43

long do you think you can keep us here? Our families must have all the police in New Mexico out looking for us by this time!''

''I doubt that. I think your parents have more sense than to disobey instructions.'' Buck's eyes crinkled in amusement. ''You're a spunky little gal, aren't you? How come you're not crying like your friend here?'' He gestured toward Jesse, whose shoulders were heaving with silent sobs.

Marianne ignored the question. ''I want to know what you are planning to do with us.''

''Well, seeing as how you've asked me so nicely . . .'' Buck paused for effect, as though considering the possibilities. ''I could tie you up and pile you in the corner. That would save me from having to watch you all night. Or I could lock you in the storeroom off the kitchen. It would be pretty cold out there, away from the fire and all.'' He waited a moment for her reaction.

Marianne regarded him coldly. Her face did not change expression.

''Or,'' Buck continued slowly, ''I might decide that you are smart enough to know that your best bet is to cooperate. I have a gun and the keys to the station wagon. If I let you all walk out of here right now, there wouldn't be anyplace for you to go. The closest town is a good twenty miles from here. You'd freeze to death before you made it on foot with no more clothes than you have. We're up about eleven thousand feet, you know.''

''If we do cooperate,'' Glenn said, ''if we agree not to make trouble, will we be allowed to sleep in the bunk rooms with the doors open for heat?''

''I might consider it.'' Buck was enjoying himself.

Jesse lowered her hands from her face. ''You are going to let us go, aren't you? I mean, later.''

Bruce gave up trying to eat. With an effort he swallowed the food that was in his mouth and laid the fork on his plate. He felt his hands clenching into fists as he awaited the answer.

"Of course, you'll go home. What do you think we want to do, adopt you? A great family we'd make, Rita and me, and our five lovely kids, and dear Uncle Juan dropping in to visit every now and then." He grinned at her.

Rita, coming in to stand beside him, was not smiling. "Stop joking around with them, Buck. There's no reason to."

"We might as well enjoy our little visitors." He turned his grin upon her. "What's the matter with you, anyway? You getting jealous?"

"Jealous!" Rita stared at him. "What are you talking about?"

"Of this little blond spitfire here? She is pretty cute. I like to see a girl with spirit."

"Now wait a minute." Dexter stiffened in his seat.

But Glenn was already on his feet. "You watch the way you talk about these girls! You don't have any right—"

"You forget, buddy boy, I have a pistol. It gives me a right to do anything I want to do." The amusement was gone from Buck's voice. "Sit down."

Glenn did not move. Standing there in the firelight, his shoulders a broad silhouette against the glow, his strong young body straight with defiance, he seemed to Bruce to be a kind of god, a symbol of courage and strength, one step above mortal men.

"Pistol or no pistol, you leave the girls alone!"

"Glenn." Marianne's eyes widened in horror. "Don't do anything." She clutched at his arm. "Please!"

LOIS DUNCAN

"He's not going to insult you girls! There aren't going to be any compromises in that direction. That has to be understood." Reluctantly he allowed himself to be drawn down into his seat.

"He's right, Buck." There was a flatness to Rita's voice. "You leave those girls alone. That's not part of this."

"I am the one who makes the rules around here," Buck said coldly. His eyes were on Glenn. "You're going to make trouble once too often, son. As it is, you've talked yourself and your buddies into a night in the storeroom. Get back there now. If you're lucky, you may find a couple of blankets back there."

Dexter threw a quick glance at Jesse. "Can't the girls sleep in the bunk room? You know they won't make trouble."

Marianne's chin was set. "I don't want to sleep here. I'd rather freeze with the rest of you."

"You'll do what you're told." Buck's decision was made. "You three boys, get into the storeroom. Girls, you help Rita clear the table."

Bruce got up obediently. His original terror had turned to numbness.

Jesse reached over and touched his hand. "We'll see you in the morning, Brucie."

It was a silly thing to say, but the touch was comforting, and the fact that it was Jesse, pale-faced and trembling herself, who had thought to say it.

Glenn was looking at Marianne. "You'll be okay?"

"Yes."

"Get a move on," Buck said, and Bruce hesitated, waiting for some sign from his brother.

Instead, it was Dexter who, with a gesture foreign to

46

him, put an arm around the younger boy's shoulders and said, "Come on, fellow, it can't be as bad in there as they make it out to be," and walked with him, through the warmth of the kitchen, into the little room filled with darkness and cold.

Chapter Four

The calls began at six o'clock.

For Mrs. French, the telephone was ringing when she opened the front door. Pausing in the hallway to remove her coat and gloves, she called, "Jesse, will you get that, dear?"

There was no answer, and the phone continued ringing.

"Jesse!" Mrs. French called again, and then, with a shrug of loving impatience, muttering, "That girl—probably in her room reading or so deep in her daydreams she doesn't even hear it," she hurried into the living room.

The telephone was on a table in the corner, and she plucked the receiver from the hook with one hand while removing her hat with the other.

"Hello?"

There was a pause, and then a voice asked, "Mrs. French?"

"Yes." She was disentangling the hat from a bobby pin which was holding it and dropped it onto the table. "This is she."

"I'm calling about your daughter."

"About Jesse?" The statement caught her by surprise. "What about her? Who is this anyway?"

"Just a friend," the voice said. "Someone who wants to be sure your daughter comes back to you safely. By this time you must know that she is gone."

"Gone? Jesse?" Automatically Mrs. French's eyes flew to the curving stairway that led to the second floor. "I don't know what you mean. Gone where?"

"A long way from here," said the voice. "To a place where she will not be found. I am the one who can bring her back to you safely."

Mrs. French shook her head in disbelief. "I don't know who you are, but you must be crazy. Jesse hasn't gone anywhere. She is upstairs in her room."

"Are you sure," asked the voice. "Have you looked? Have you seen her since school let out this afternoon?"

"No, but I just got home myself. I was at a committee meeting of the Officers' Wives Club. I'm sure . . ." Abruptly Mrs. French dropped the receiver onto the table. "Jesse!" she called. "Jesse, come down here!"

Without pausing for an answer, she crossed the living room to the stairs and started up them.

"Jesse!"

Several moments went by before she returned to the telephone. Her hand was trembling as she picked up the receiver. When she spoke, her voice was very low. "Where is Jesse? What have you done with my daughter?"

"Fifteen thousand dollars!" Rod Donavan exclaimed incredulously. "Why, that's impossible! I don't have that kind of money!"

"You can get it," the voice said. "That is, if seeing the girl again is important to you."

"If it's important!" Mr. Donavan forced his voice into control. "Look here, now, how do I know that Marianne is with you? I want you to let her speak to me."

"That is impossible."

"Why is it impossible? If you have hurt her . . ."

"She isn't hurt, Mr. Donavan. Not yet anyway. She is not here to speak to you. She is being held in another place. The thing for you to do is to get the money."

Mr. Donavan drew a long breath.

"If—if I can manage to get together that much money somehow, where do you want me to take it? How do I get it to you?"

"Don't worry about that," the voice told him. "You just get the money, and I'll let you know what to do with it. Oh, and another thing, it would be a mistake for you to call the police. A very bad mistake."

"Well, let me tell you something, whoever you are," Rod Donavan said tightly. "When you call again to tell me where to bring the money, you have Marianne there at the telephone. I want to hear her voice, and I want to hear her tell me that she is unharmed. If Marianne doesn't speak to me, I will know that this is a trick, that you don't have her at all. In that case you will not get a single penny."

There was a pause, and then the voice said, "It is not you who are making the rules, Mr. Donavan. You will do what I tell you if you want to see the girl again. What I tell you now is to get the money and stay at home and wait until I call you."

There was a click, and the wire went blank.

Rod Donavan stood holding the receiver, listening to the

sudden silence on the other end of the wire. Then he lowered it slowly and replaced it on the hook.

From the kitchen his wife called, "Rod, was that Marianne? Is she at somebody's house? I can't imagine what is making her so late."

"No, it wasn't Marianne. I'll tell you about it in a minute." Rod stood unmoving, staring at the telephone. Then, on impulse, he lifted the hook and dialed a number.

"Hello, Steve? This is Rod Donavan. I wonder, can your boy Glenn come to the telephone?"

"Why, no, Rod," Mr. Kirtland said, surprised. "Glenn hasn't come home yet. Was there something you needed to talk to him about?"

"No, not really. I just wondered if he'd got home all right. It's several hours since school let out. You're . . . well, you're not worried about him, are you?"

"Worried? Good grief, no." Mr. Kirtland was amused at the question. "Glenn has so many activities he seldom gets home much before dinnertime. Today I think he went over to the garage to pick up his car. He's been having it painted. Say, Rod"—he was frankly curious—"what is all this about anyway? Is something the matter?"

"I don't know. I just wanted to check on something. You haven't received any phone calls from him or about him?"

"Not unless he called his mother before I got home. Come to think of it, Bruce isn't home yet either. Now, that is kind of funny. Bruce always takes the school bus."

"Glenn took the bus today, too," Rod Donavan said quietly. "I stopped by the school this afternoon and saw him through the bus window. He was sitting with Marianne."

"Funny. I guess he got off at some other stop. Maybe he went home with a friend or something. Anyway he'll be coming in soon. That's one thing you can count on with our boys.'' Mr. Kirtland laughed good-naturedly. ''Neither one of them would miss dinner.''

''Well, look,'' Mr. Donavan said slowly, ''I want you to do something for me. If you should receive a phone call from Glenn, or about him, or Bruce . . .''

''What are you being so mysterious about?'' Mr. Kirtland was beginning to be impatient. ''I don't understand what it is you want to know. Hasn't Marianne come home yet, is that it? You think she's gone someplace with Glenn?''

''Just phone me,'' Rod Donavan said, ''if Glenn comes home or if you have any communication about him. Please.''

''All right. Sure, if you want me to.'' Mr. Kirtland hung up in bewilderment.

His wife, who had been reading the paper, glanced up with interest. ''What on earth was that all about?''

Mr. Kirtland shook his head. ''Darned if I know. It was Rod Donavan, Marian's new husband. I wonder if he has a screw loose or something.''

''Heavens, why?'' Mrs. Kirtland laid down the paper. ''He may not be a dynamo like Jack Paget, but he seems normal enough. What was that about Marianne's being with Glenn? It wouldn't be surprising. All the girls follow Glenn around as though he were the Pied Piper.''

''He said to phone him if we hear from Glenn. Or if we get another kind of phone call. I couldn't make out what he meant.''

''I can't imagine . . .'' Mrs. Kirtland began.

It was then that the telephone rang.

Mark Crete was not at home when the phone rang in his bedroom.

Mr. Crete was a forty-year-old bachelor with a time-consuming social life which he had not tried to alter in any major way when his nephew came to live with him.

"I am not the father type," he had said, and none of his friends had disagreed with him. The statement was too true to be argued.

The telephone rang at half hour intervals all evening. It was a quarter past three when Mark Crete finally pulled into the driveway. He left his car parked there, not bothering to put it in the garage, and went into the house.

He did not stop at Dexter's room. He did not stop anywhere; he went straight to his bedroom and, pausing only long enough to remove his shoes, tumbled wearily onto his bed.

After a few minutes he stirred himself enough to get up and run a glass of water. He drank it and then, leaving the bathroom light burning, he returned to his room.

With a gigantic yawn he lowered himself to the bed for the second time and then, on impulse, reached out and flicked the switch on the bedside telephone, shutting it off for the rest of the night.

Chapter Five

Dexter was worried about Jesse.

It was strange that he should be, for he really did not know her at all. There had been that moment on the bus when he had looked across the aisle and noticed in her, for an instant, a resemblance to someone he had once known. Then in the car she had been crying. He had not worried about her then because it was a natural thing for a girl to cry. It was a good deal more natural, in his opinion, than to sit there like Marianne, as controlled as though being kidnapped were only another event in the course of an average week. If Jesse had kept on crying, if she had wept and shrieked and become hysterical, he would have accepted and understood it.

But she did not.

Instead, she became quiet. It was not a normal quiet; it was a kind of dead stillness, as though a light had been switched off inside her.

Dexter noticed it in the morning when they were released from the storeroom and allowed at last to stand in the front room by the fire.

The night had been the longest and most miserable of his life. The cold of the storeroom had been as complete as the inside of a refrigerator. The saving grace had been finding the sleeping bags. There were six of them, stacked in a pile against the far wall, and they had found them by touch, as they groped about in the darkness for the promised blankets.

"If it hadn't been for them," he told the girls later, "we would never have lived through the night," and Marianne nodded.

"I'll never forget how cold it was in the morning when I went in to bring you coffee. I unbolted the door, and the cold seemed to come rushing out to meet me. I was afraid to look."

She had come in about eight with the coffee and a package of buns, which evidently were to constitute breakfast.

"I can't let you out," she had whispered. "Buck's gone somewhere, and he told Rita you were to stay in here until he came back. I talked her into letting me bring you these. Are you all right?"

"I guess so," Glenn had muttered, and then the door had been locked again, and they had been left to huddle in the sleeping bags until, according to Bruce's wristwatch, close to noon.

When they were released at last and allowed to move into the living room, Dexter glanced about for Jesse. She was not in the living room, so when he had warmed himself a little, he went into the bunk room. She was standing by the window. Her back was toward him, and she did not turn when he came to stand beside her.

"Hi," he said awkwardly. "How did it go? Did you and Marianne make it through the night all right?"

Without looking at him, Jesse nodded.

"Did that guy Buck bother you or anything?"

"No."

Dexter wished that she would turn so that he could see her face.

"Did you eat any breakfast?" he asked.

"Yes."

He could tell she was lying. "You didn't really, did you? Jesse, you have to eat"

"Oh, please . . ." She did turn then and face him, and he saw the strange look in her eyes, as though shock and fright had wiped away all emotion. Something has happened, he thought. Something more than I know about.

Impulsively he reached out and touched her hand and was startled at how cold it was.

"Jesse," he said, "come in by the fire."

"No."

"You're cold. You shouldn't be in here by the window."

"Please," she said, "can't you just leave me alone?"

It was the sort of thing he himself would have said under the same circumstances. He had, in fact, said it himself in both words and actions, many times. Now, with a feeling of helplessness, he obeyed her wishes and left her by the window and went into the other room.

Marianne was seated on the floor by the fireplace. She had evidently spent the morning exploring the cabinets and shelves in the bunk room, for she had located a pile of paperback books, a deck of cards, and a checkerboard, although there did not seem to be any checkers.

Glenn, who had crouched beside her to look over the pile of articles, asked, "Where did you get all this?"

"Just dug them out. Whoever uses this cabin for hunting must have kept them here for entertainment in the evenings. Rita didn't mind my looking. In fact, she took some of the books herself."

They were automatically keeping their voices low, so that they would not carry to the kitchen, where, through the open door, they could see Buck at the counter, eating and talking to Rita.

"Do you know where he went?" Bruce asked softly, and Marianne nodded.

"Down to that little town, the one we came through on our way up here last night. He was going to phone Juan. I guess that's the closest place there is a telephone."

Dexter's voice was low. "What's the matter with Jesse?"

"The matter with her? Why, the same thing that's the matter with all of us, I guess. She wants to go home."

"It's more than that," Dexter persisted. "She wasn't like this last night. She was scared and upset, sure, but not to the extent that she is now. Something must have happened."

"I don't know what," Marianne told him. "We slept in the second bedroom last night, and when we got up this morning, Buck had already left. Rita hasn't even talked to us. She has been sitting in the kitchen all morning, reading and drinking coffee."

"If Juan phoned our families," Glenn said, "they must have made their plans by now. I wish we knew what the score was."

Marianne nodded. "Shall we ask him?"

"I'll do it. The worst Buck can do is refuse to answer." Glenn got up and went across the room to the kitchen.

Bruce's eyes followed him admiringly. "He's not afraid of anybody."

Dexter, too, watched the tall boy, noting the width of his shoulders, the ease of his stride. "What's it like to have Superman for a brother?"

Bruce accepted the question as a compliment. "It's great. Everybody likes Glenn."

I don't, thought Dexter. He did not speak the words aloud, but Marianne saw them in his eyes.

"Everybody likes him," she said pointedly, "unless they happen to be jealous of him."

Dexter was immediately on the defensive. "What is that supposed to mean?"

"If you don't know," said Marianne, "it's possible it doesn't apply."

"You're darned right, it doesn't apply! If you think I'm jealous of Glenn Kirtland, that I'd change places for one minute with him or with anyone like him—" He stopped his tirade with effort.

"What are you talking about?" Bruce asked innocently. "Nobody's jealous of Glenn. He wouldn't let them be. He's so nice to everybody."

Before the honest bewilderment in his voice, Dexter felt a sudden shame at his outburst.

"Sure he is, Brucie," he said apologetically to the younger boy. "I didn't mean that. I don't know why I said it."

To his surprise Marianne reacted identically. "I baited you into it. I'm sorry, Dex. I was being horrid." She glanced down at her hands, clenched in her lap, and slowly forced herself to open them. "The tension is getting to all of us. We're going to end up clawing and biting each other."

At that moment, Glenn came out of the kitchen and joined the group at the fire.

"He says the wheels are turning," he said, seating himself on the floor beside Marianne. "There is one family he hasn't been able to contact. Buck wants to wait to pick up the money until he can get it from everybody. Then he'll release all of us at once."

"The one they haven't reached is my uncle," Dexter said with certainty. "He's never home. He probably hasn't even noticed that I'm missing."

Marianne regarded him with wonder. "But surely, when you didn't come home to dinner?"

"He usually eats his dinner out. I cook for myself." Dexter said defensively, "I'm a good cook."

Marianne seemed shocked. "But doesn't your mother?"

"My mother's dead." He got up then and left them by the fire and went into the bedroom to Jesse.

She was standing, just as he had left her, by the window, gazing out into the vista of trees and sleet gray sky.

Dexter stood beside her a moment and said, "Glenn talked to Buck. We're going to be out of here soon." When Jesse didn't answer, he continued, "Juan phoned our families last night. There's just one he hasn't reached, and I think it's mine. As soon as he gets hold of my uncle and makes arrangements to pick up the money . . ."

His voice faded out before her lack of response. For a short while they stood in silence.

Then Jesse asked, "Why did you come in here?"

He was disconcerted by the question. "I don't know exactly. I guess I just—"

"Yes?"

"Just wanted to talk."

"You could have talked to the others," Jesse said.

"I know. I didn't just want to talk to be talking. I wanted to talk to you."

The words were true. The realization of their truth startled him. He wanted to be with this girl. He, Dexter, the loner, who hadn't wanted to be with anybody for so long, who hadn't cared about anybody for so long. And why? Why, suddenly, now? And why this girl, whom he hardly knew?

Yet he did know her. He knew the straight set of the narrow shoulders, the fine, clean curve of the neck beneath the smooth dark hair. She was still turned away from him, and he ached to reach out and draw her around to face him.

"I know you," he wanted to say. "I know you!"

Was it because, physically, she resembled the girl in New York? Yes, undoubtedly that was part of it, yet there was more. Now, as he stood beside her, he had the strange feeling that if he could turn her toward him and look into her eyes, he would see something there that was a reflection of his own.

> I met myself the other day,
> In quiet mouth, in eyes of gray—

Where had he heard that poem? It must have been from his mother. Everything he knew of poetry had come from her.

When he pictured his mother, it was always on the sofa in the living room of their New York apartment, with her legs curled under her like a little girl, reading poetry. During that terrible year when he had been sick, and all of the time afterward, when he was learning to walk again, when he was slowly starting to get some life back into his right side, she had read to him. The time had gone by faster, somehow, and it had been more bearable. When he thought back upon it now, of that painful, frustrating time, he remembered it with all of his senses—the taste of his own angry tears of exhaustion, the smell of hospitals, the feel of his father's strong hands, patiently kneading and working the useless muscles of his leg and shoulder. And always in the background, the sound of his mother's voice, reading.

That time was like another life, like a little segment of another world, complete in itself, with just the three of them, bound together in perfect closeness by agony and love. It had been another thing altogether when he was well enough to start school again, to break from the protection of his private world and brave the cruel normality of the public school system.

Thanks to his mother's tutoring, he was not behind his age-group academically. In fact, if anything, he was ahead. It was the social side of life, the easy, joking give-and-take of his classmates, that was more than he could handle.

"I'm different!" he had exclaimed wretchedly to his parents. "They don't like me because I'm different!"

"We're all different," his father had said.

"But my difference shows! Nobody wants me on their side at games. I can't run fast enough."

"You're good at other things," his mother had reminded him. "Your reading is way ahead of your grade level. Your teacher told me."

"But my handwriting isn't. I have to do it with my left hand."

"So who cares?" His mother had smiled at him. "Everybody has his own problems. Most of us are so involved with our own that we don't even notice anyone else's. So you limp a little, so your handwriting isn't perfect. What does it matter? Nobody cares but you!"

The love in her voice had made the words believable.

How eagerly he had grasped at them, ready to accept them as true.

Nobody notices, he had told himself. Nobody cares.

He had lived for three years like that, in his own little dreamworld. He had worked, during those years, and he had improved physically. He had conquered the limp, except when he was particularly tired, and had exercised regularly, even learning to ski. Although he never developed much coordination with his right hand, he did improve with practice his use of the left one, and his script, although never beautiful, was at least possible to read. The underdeveloped arm and shoulder muscles he concealed with long-sleeved shirts and sweaters, and he convinced himself that nobody was aware of them.

Until the girl.

She was the first girl he had ever loved, and he had loved her with the complete concentration of purpose that was his primary characteristic. He had thought she felt the same way about him. He had thought it, anyway, until that summer afternoon when he had overheard her: *"He's a nice guy and all that, and cute enough in a jacket, but I think I'd die if I ever had to be seen on the beach with him!"*

She had laughed when she said it, that low, lovely laugh which could tie his stomach in knots, and he had stood there, stunned, unable to move. And then he had turned and walked away, and he had never called her or spoken to her again.

At home that night he had not told his parents. He had left his dinner uneaten and gone straight to bed.

"It's a touch of stomach flu or something," he had told his mother when she hovered over him. "I'll be okay tomorrow."

She had leaned over to touch his forehead. "You don't have any fever."

"I said, I'll be all right."

He had turned his face away, and his mother had said helplessly, "It's probably just the heat. It has been such a hot summer."

She had been hurt, and he had known it. But he himself was too hurt to care.

"Go away!" he had told her. "I don't need you! I don't need anybody!" And after she had left him, he had lain there in the hot apartment with his face pressed into his pillow and cried until there were no tears left to shed.

Then he had slept.

When he got up the next morning, he had changed. It was funny how quickly the change had come. It was as though while he slept, there had grown about him a wall, a transparent wall through which he could see but through which no one and nothing could reach him.

When he passed the girl in the hall that morning, he had ignored her. He had looked past her, as though she were not worth the trouble of seeing. When she tried to speak to him, he had pretended not to hear her.

I don't need you, he had thought, and afterward he had wondered if he had spoken it aloud, so violently were the words churning within him. I don't need you.

I don't need anybody!

"I met myself the other day . . ." He wished he could think of the rest of the poem. It was strange that he should have remembered it through the years. *I met myself*. What was it about Jesse that he should feel as though he had found himself in her? What was it that he recognized, that had drawn him in here, aching with an emptiness that nothing, ever, could possibly fill?

"Jesse."

His emotions must have shown in his voice, for to his surprise, she did turn around. She stood there directly before him, her face raised to his, and the blank look was gone. Her eyes were pools of pure terror.

"Dex," she whispered, "I didn't want to tell you. I didn't want to tell any of you because knowing it won't do any good. It's all terrible enough without—without . . ."

Her voice trailed off, and he asked, "What is it?"

"I didn't want to tell, but I have to. I have to tell it to somebody!"

"What is it?" Dexter demanded. He found suddenly that he was gripping her shoulders with both hands. "Tell me!"

"Last night," said Jesse, "I couldn't sleep. I guess none of us could very well. Marianne did doze off after a while; I could hear the change in her breathing. I lay there in my bunk, and I was scared, and I hadn't had any dinner. All at once the whole room seemed to be spinning. I knew I had to have a drink of water. I remembered the pitcher of water out in the kitchen, and I thought I would get some."

"Yes?" Dexter's hands were still on her shoulders.

"Our door was partly open so the heat from the fire could come in. I thought that Buck and Rita had gone to bed in the other bunk room. But they hadn't. They were in the living room, sitting in front of the fire. They were drinking beer or something. The whole room was full of the smell of it. And they were talking. I stood there in the doorway, and they didn't know I was there, and I heard what they were saying."

She paused. When Dexter did not speak, she continued. "Rita was asking about the bus driver, Mr. Godfrey. She wanted to know what they had done with him. Buck told her . . . they killed him. That sweet old man. They killed him, Dexter! They killed him!''

For a long moment they stood there, locked together in the horror of it.

Then Jesse drew in a long breath and took the final step of reason. ''They've already killed one person, Dexter. What are they going to do to us?''

Chapter Six

"So they did kill him," Glenn said slowly. "It figures."

"You don't seem too surprised," said Dexter.

"To tell the truth, I'm not. There was something Buck said on the bus about Juan's having used the gun before. And he shut Rita up so quickly when she started asking questions in front of us. They must have done something with Godfrey in order to get Buck into the driver's seat, and . . . well . . ." He nodded thoughtfully. "It all adds up."

He had wondered what the matter was when Jesse came out of the back room, looking as though the world had fallen in on her, and told him, "Dex wants to see you." He had seen Marianne's open look of curiosity and Bruce's sudden movement, as though to accompany him. Then Jesse had seated herself by the fireplace, and Glenn had realized that she meant him alone, and he had risen and gone into the bunk room where Dexter waited.

The story had been a short one, and he was not surprised by it. It merely strengthened his determination about the decision he had already made.

"We are going to have to get out of here," he said.

Glenn Kirtland was never going to be paid for with ransom. From the very beginning his mind had refused even to consider the possibility. The disgrace of the situation was more intolerable than the danger. Glenn Kirtland, leader of the student body. Glenn Kirtland, captain of the football team. Glenn Kirtland, hero of the campus, 170 pounds of solid, well-coordinated muscle, snatched up and kidnapped like a baby! The helplessness of the image was infuriating.

And it wasn't as though there were a group of strong-arm gangsters. True, in the beginning there had been two men, but Juan, for all practical purposes, was no longer part of the picture. There was only one man, well built, of course, but no better so than Glenn, and one squatty little woman. The difference was the pistol. Glenn ground his teeth when he thought of the pistol. To think that one small weapon could carry with it the power to hold five people captive!

"If we could only get our hands on the gun . . ." he began slowly, and Dexter said, "We can't. I've thought about it, and there's no way. He always has it with him. He wears it under his jacket."

"What about at night when he's sleeping?"

"I imagine he keeps that pistol where he can reach it. Besides, Rita's right in the room with him. It wouldn't do us much good, anyway, when we're locked up in the storeroom."

"The girls aren't," said Glenn. "Marianne's a light-footed little thing. If there were any way of slipping in there and getting the pistol, I bet she could find it."

"You'd let her do that!" Dexter stared at him in amazement. "What if she got caught?"

"If she got caught, she'd get caught. There's nothing to lose by chancing it. We wouldn't be any worse off than we were before."

"No." Dexter shook his head decidedly. "We don't know what Buck might do, if he woke up suddenly and found her there. Especially with the gun right there. My gosh, Glenn, she's your girl. I don't see how you could consider asking her to do that."

"Let's take it by force then," Glenn said determinedly. "There are three of us fellows. You and I are seniors, and Bruce is little, but he's wiry. We could all rush Buck together."

"Somebody would be sure to get hurt," said Dexter. "Maybe even killed. Fists don't add up to much against a gun."

"If we found something we could use for a weapon . . ."

"There isn't one. Marianne plowed through this whole cabin this morning and didn't come up with anything more dangerous than a checkerboard."

"Well, you suggest something then!" There was exasperation in Glenn's voice. "If you don't think my ideas are worth trying, what do you have to offer in their place? We're agreed we have to get out of here. That means a battle of some kind."

"Not necessarily," Dexter said slowly. "I think we could cut out of here while they are sleeping. Just get in the station wagon and take off down the mountain."

"And where are you going to get the car keys?" Glenn asked skeptically. "Do you plan to walk up to Buck and ask for them? He keeps them in his pants pocket, and it would be just as hard to get them away from him as it would be to get the pistol.''

"Maybe we could start it without the keys," said Dexter. "It's a Chevy station wagon and not a new one. How old would you say it is?''

"I don't know. Maybe four or five years old.''

"I might be able to start it by crossing some wires in the ignition.''

"Do you think you could?'' Glenn regarded him with grudging respect. "How much time would it take you to do it?''

"I'd have to look the thing over to know. It would be easy if I had tools. As it is, I'll have to try to make do with a penknife. Of course, there's the matter of getting out there. Buck locked us up last night, so I imagine he'll do it tonight, too. I wonder if Buck has the storeroom key on the same chain with the car keys.''

"I don't think so,'' said Glenn. "Remember how Marianne used it this morning when she unlocked the door to give us coffee? It's more likely Rita keeps it, and if so, Marianne probably knows where it is.''

"I'll get her aside and ask her.'' Dexter got up from the bunk on which he had been sitting. "You sit down with Bruce and let him in on the scene, and I'll tell Jesse. We shouldn't all be seen talking together. They might suspect we were planning something.''

"Hey. Hold it a minute.'' Glenn stopped him with a gesture. "The girls have to be in on this, to get us out of the storeroom and everything, but you're not planning on taking them with us when we run for it, are you?''

Dexter stared at him. For a moment he was too stunned to answer. Finally he said, "Of course, I am.''

"That's crazy, Dex. We'd be finished before we started.

We might be out in that car an hour before you could get it running. What if Buck or Rita should wake up during that time and see that the girls are missing?''

"Not just the girls. We'll all be missing.''

"But they'll never look in the storeroom. We can lock it back up as though we were still in there, and there won't be any way for them to know we're gone. The girls are different. They can be checked on. All Buck has to do is walk past the door to the bunk room, and he'll see it's empty.''

"What do you expect to do about them?'' Dexter asked incredulously. "Leave them here? Take off in the car and escape without them?''

"Don't make it sound so terrible. It's not as though they wouldn't be rescued. We could stop at the first town and send the police back for them.''

"And have them here in the middle of a gunfight? Or used for hostages? You are the one who's crazy!''

"Look, fella, be sensible.'' Glenn's earnestness was persuasive. "We'll leave the girls and bring help back for them. It's the only way to do it. We'll never make it otherwise.''

"Then I'd as soon not make it,'' Dexter said decidedly. "I'm not leaving Jesse alone here with Buck. Not for one hour or even one minute. I wouldn't leave Marianne either. If you want to take your brother and run out on us, go ahead. I'm surely not going to stop you.''

"We couldn't do it without you. I couldn't get the engine started.'' Glenn made the admission ruefully. "I drive my car, sure, but I've never had time to learn much about the mechanics of it.''

"It's settled then?'' said Dexter. "We'll all make a run for it together?''

"You're calling the terms. There doesn't seem to be much choice."

They stood there for a moment, taking measure of each other, two boys who would never have joined forces under other circumstances.

It was Glenn who broke the silence. "You don't like me, do you?"

Dexter hesitated. The truth was there between them, past denying. "No," he said.

"Why not?" Glenn asked with real interest. He was not angry, only curious. He was used to being liked by everyone. His popularity was a fact of his existence, something he had come to accept as proper and inevitable.

Dexter considered the question.

"I don't know," he said slowly. "Marianne thinks I'm jealous of you. I got mad today when she said it. I guess I wouldn't have reacted so hard if it hadn't been true."

"Because I'm football captain?" Glenn nodded understandingly. "That's natural. It's a status thing, especially with the girls."

"It wasn't just that. You seemed to have everything. You were all the things I wished I could be." He paused. "I don't feel that way any longer."

"That's good." Glenn accepted the statement at face value. "If we're going to organize this escape together, we'd better be friends."

"We can't be," Dexter said quietly.

"Why not?" Glenn asked in surprise. It had not been the reaction he expected.

"Because you have to feel something to be a friend. You don't feel anything."

"You're nuts," Glenn told him. "I feel as much as anybody."

"I don't believe it. You haven't given one thought to anybody but yourself since we got up here. Oh, you've made a big show, all right, said all the right things and made all the right gestures. 'You leave those girls alone, Buck!' But when the chips are down, you'd as soon take off and leave your girl here for Buck to treat any way he wants to. That kid brother of yours is scared silly, and what the devil have you done about it? Jesse's the one who's been looking out for him. You're a taker, Kirtland. You use people. You stand there and let them adore you, and you don't give anything back to them. I bet you've never really loved anybody in your whole life!"

The statement hung there like a question. For a long moment Glenn struggled with his anger. A dozen retorts, a dozen denials occurred to him; he was tempted to offer them in a tirade to match the one that had just been delivered. But what would be the use of it, he asked himself; what would it gain him? Dexter could be handled, as everyone was handled.

Slowly, deliberately he forced himself to smile. He put amusement into his voice. "I asked you to be my friend? I'm revoking the offer. With you for a friend, I wouldn't need any enemies."

The tension was broken. Dexter's face colored with embarrassment.

"I'm sorry," he muttered awkwardly. "I didn't have any right to say that. I don't have a right to do any preaching to anybody."

"That's okay. You're keyed up. We both are." Glenn put his hand on the other boy's shoulder. It was the same gesture he had used with Bruce, the night they stood in the driveway, looking at the damaged car. "When we're out

72

of this, we'll laugh about it. It'll be an adventure. Something to talk about in the lodge after skiing."

"Sure," said Dexter. He shifted uncomfortably. "I'd better get out in the living room. Buck's going to start wondering what we're talking about for so long."

"I'm surprised he hasn't checked on us already."

When Dexter had left the room, Glenn moved over to stand by the window. Without realizing it, he assumed the same position that Jesse had earlier, his forehead against the pane, his eyes on the trees and the sky beyond them.

It had begun to snow. A layer of white was forming at the window ledge, and the ground appeared in dark patches where the flakes had not yet thickened.

I could hike my way out of here, Glenn told himself.

He toyed with the idea, letting his mind run over it. It was twenty miles, Buck had told them, to the nearest town. That was twenty miles by winding trail, but it would be shorter straight down the side of the mountain. I could make it, Glenn thought, if I had the right clothing—boots and parka or a heavy jacket like the one Buck wears. The others couldn't do it, but I could. I could make it!

For an instant he was tempted. The idea of starting out alone to brave the elements was pleasing to him. He was in good shape physically; his well-built body was conditioned by hours of football practice and skiing. There would certainly be some glory in having hiked one's way to freedom, in being the valiant escapee who defied danger to send back help to the others.

Or would it look as though he had run out on the others? Dexter's use of that term bothered him. It was one thing to be a hero who had outwitted his adversaries, but quite another to be looked upon as a deserter of girls and a younger brother. When help did arrive, it was doubtful that they would still be here. Buck would hardly be sitting, waiting for the rescuers. As soon as he discovered that Glenn was missing, he would pack the others into the station wagon and take off into Colorado or down into Mexico. There would be no possibility of finding them then, and it was conceivable that Glenn might be considered to blame for this.

No, Dexter's plan was better. Much as it irked him, he had to admit it. If only it didn't make him so completely dependent upon the other boy's ability. What he wouldn't give to be able to doctor the blasted ignition himself! But mechanical know-how was not one of his fortes. Whenever something went wrong with his own automobile, he put it into the garage and let the experts take care of it.

The whole thing was ironical. If his car had not been in the shop, he would not be here today, and in all probability Marianne would not be either. They would have taken off after school in the Thunderbird and left the creaky old bus to drag its way home without them. But the car had had to be fixed, and as quickly as possible; there would have been hell to pay if anybody had got a look at that fender.

Of course, Bruce had seen it. That had been unfortunate. There had been a few rocky moments there when the kid started asking questions: *"What happened? . . . But don't you have to report accidents? Won't they have to know, at the garage, that it was reported?"*

But handling Bruce was no problem. All you had to do was buddy him. That was one thing about having a kid brother who thought the sun rose and set on you. You smiled at him and patted him on the shoulder, and he would run and fetch for you till his legs fell off and be grateful for the opportunity.

It was different with Dexter. He couldn't quite make

Dexter out; something about the guy made him vaguely uncomfortable. That tirade, for instance, about feeling things. That was a crazy subject for a person to get steamed up about. He personally couldn't care less about the way Dexter felt about things. Why couldn't everybody just take the world as it came and stop getting emotional about it?

Yet there was one thing the boy had said which bothered him. That part about not loving. *I bet you've never really loved anybody in your whole life!*

Glenn had wondered about that sometimes. Other people did seem to get so involved with each other. Many of his friends had girls they were ''in love'' with; they bumbled around with stars in their eyes and fawning expressions on their faces.

To Glenn, it seemed incredible that any one person could hold a position of so much importance to another. He dated, of course; he liked girls, especially pretty ones. That was the reason he took Marianne out so often. He had even said, ''I love you,'' on certain occasions, when the situation seemed to warrant that the words be spoken. But he had never felt deeply enough about any girl to look beneath the surface, to try to find out what she was really like as a person. And he never wasted emotion by thinking about any of them after the brief romances were over.

With a shrug, he dismissed the problem. ''What does it matter? Someday it will happen. I just haven't run across a great enough girl yet, that's all.

He stood for a while longer, watching the snow falling. If there was a lack somewhere within himself, it was one of which he was not aware.

Chapter Seven

The story about the missing school bus and driver was in the morning paper.

"So that's the way it was done!" Rod Donavan finished reading the last paragraph and crumpled the page angrily in his fists. "This crazy Godfrey reaches the end of the run and simply keeps going. He must be insane!"

"His wife doesn't think so," said Marian Donavan. "She thinks that something has happened to him. If she had any idea that he were involved in a kidnapping, she certainly wouldn't have reported to the police that he didn't come home last night."

Her voice was thin with exhaustion, her eyes swollen from a night of weeping. Her husband regarded her with concern.

"I wish you'd lie down for a little, Marian. You know I'll call you the minute there's any communication."

"I can't. Not now. Perhaps after Jack calls." She paused and then added, "If he does call. He must have had my message by this time. Do you suppose he is just not answering?''

''You left word that it was an emergency and had to do with one of the children. He couldn't ignore that.''

''You don't know Jack. If he were busy with something, or partying, or just in one of those happy-go-lucky moods of his . . .'' She raised her hands and pressed them against her forehead. ''He has to call! He has to give us the money! After all, Marianne is his own daughter.''

''She never forgets it, that's for sure.'' There was a hint of bitterness in Rod's voice. ''It's been Daddy this and Daddy that, 'Daddy always used to say,' and 'Daddy never did things that way' until sometimes I've wanted to shake her, to shout at her, 'If your Daddy was as wonderful as all that, why did he walk off and leave you?' ''

''You wouldn't,'' Marian Donavan said confidently. ''You'd never say a thing like that to one of the children.''

''Of course, I wouldn't, not when you've worked so hard to build their father up to them. Sometimes I think it would have been better for you to have told them the truth about him in the first place, to have said, 'Your father was an irresponsible bounder, a charming sort of Peter Pan guy who never grew up. He went into marriage for the fun of it, because it was a new experience, and then, when he got tired of it, he simply walked out.' ''

''I want them never to know that,'' Mrs. Donavan said quietly. ''He's their father, Rod. Children need to respect their parents. They need to feel loved by them.''

''I'd like them to feel loved by *me*,'' Rod said wearily. ''Sometimes it seems so hopeless. The boys like me. There's no problem there. It's Marianne I can't get through to. The thing that kills me is that—darn it, Marian—she's just the daughter I would have wanted if I'd gone out and picked her! When I look at her, it's like seeing you, the part of you I missed by not knowing you at seventeen.''

"Oh, she looks the way I did,'' Mrs. Donavan told him, "but the resemblance ends there. I was never so lively, so vital. Marianne has a—a kind of spunkiness.''

"That is the thing that's going to pull her through this.'' Her husband reached over and took her hand. "Marianne is stubborn, darling. Nobody is going to walk on her, no matter what. If she can hold out against me for as long as she has, she can hold strong against anything. She's not going to go to pieces or do anything foolish. Wherever she is, whatever is happening, Marianne is all right. We've got to keep believing that, that she is all right.''

"The thing I don't understand,'' muttered Steve Kirtland, "is why our boys should be the ones taken, our boys and the Paget girl. Granted, we are from a good area and might be expected to be able to pay a healthy ransom, but there must be plenty of other well-to-do families in Albuquerque. Why our youngsters and ours only?''

"We don't know that there aren't others,'' said Mrs. Kirtland. "If Rod hadn't phoned us last night, we would never have realized that Marianne was missing. Perhaps the bus was filled with children, and all the parents have been warned, as we have, not to report to the police.''

"I still think we should call them. We should have done it last night as soon as we got that phone call. We could ask them to keep it quiet, not to let the reporters get hold of it.''

"But they might! Look at the story of the school bus and Mr. Godfrey's being missing! It's all over the front

78

page of the *Journal*! It's not worth the risk, Steve! If they think the police are informed, they may be afraid to return the children!''

"I know. I know. Don't you think I haven't hashed through every angle of it? Lord, what a hellish night, waiting until the bank opened this morning so I could get the money.''

"You were able to get the whole amount? We didn't have it in our account.''

"I borrowed it against our securities. There wasn't any problem. Now all we have to do is wait for a phone call telling us what to do with it." Steve Kirtland frowned thoughtfully. "I wonder . . .''

"What?''

"That thing you said a minute ago, about there possibly being others. How many kids from Valley Gardens attend the public high school?''

"I don't know. There's a good little group of them. I see them, sometimes, waiting at the bus stop.''

"Our two and the Paget girl. Who else? Think hard now. Don't the Lindleys have children?''

"Yes, two girls, but they don't ride the bus on Thursdays. Mrs. Lindley always drives in to pick them up after Pep Club." Mrs. Kirtland paused. "There's Joan Miller. She's in Bruce's class. You don't think she could be missing?''

Mr. Kirtland's jaw was set. "It will take one phone call to find out.''

He was already dialing when his wife stopped him.

"Oh, Steve, maybe we shouldn't! Not with their boy in the hospital. When the phone rings, they might think . . .''

"We have to know." Ignoring her protests, Mr. Kirtland spoke abruptly into the receiver. "Hello? Mrs. Miller?

This is Steve Kirtland, up on the hill. I'm sorry to bother you at a time like this, but I'm calling about your daughter. Is she in school today?''

There was a long pause while he listened to the voice on the other end of the wire. Then, slowly, he nodded.

"Yes. Well, I'm glad. That's—that's wonderful. . . . I know how relieved you must be. . . . They don't have anything to go on, huh? He didn't even see the car that hit him? . . . Well, you can be grateful for that anyway. A close call. Criminal. I know how you must be feeling." He struggled for an instant with his voice. "After all, our kids are . . . all we have. I mean, when you come right down to it, material things don't have much meaning . . . yes, well, thank you, Mrs. Miller. No, I wasn't calling for any special reason. I just thought—well, we wanted to know how things were going. Thank you. Good-bye."

He replaced the receiver on the hook.

"Well?" Mrs. Kirtland leaned forward eagerly.

"Their girl is in school today," Mr. Kirtland said flatly. "She didn't attend yesterday. In fact, this is the first day she has been in school since Monday. The whole family has been spending their time at the hospital."

"The boy is better?"

"He's past the crisis. They had thought they were going to lose him. Good grief, how quickly these things can happen! One moment there's a happy kid on a motorscooter. The next moment he's smashed all over the highway! Our own boys, laughing, joking around at breakfast . . . and hours later, God knows where."

"Glenn is so big and strong. He can take care of himself anywhere." The hope in Mrs. Kirtland's voice carried a note of desperation. "He'll take care of Brucie."

"Sure. Sure, he will. Glenn can always handle things."

"Oh, Steve." She closed her eyes, as though suddenly too tired to hold them open any longer. Her husband came to her and put his arms around her.

When he spoke again, it was almost a whisper. "It's not the kidnapping alone that you are afraid of. It's not just the danger to the boys. It's something else too, isn't it?"

Wordlessly, she nodded.

"It's Glenn, isn't it? You're afraid of Glenn?"

"How do you know? We've never said it. How do you know?"

"You're afraid he will use that bigness and strength to save himself. That he will get away somehow. And leave Bruce."

"How do you know?" She opened her eyes to stare at him. "I've thought it was just my—"

"He is my son, too, dear."

"I never thought you noticed. He is so handsome, so strong, so wonderful in so many ways. Yet sometimes, when I'm close to him, when I give him a hug or kiss him, I look into his eyes—and there's nothing in them. I mean, he has beautiful eyes, but they're empty." She shuddered. "I'm being silly. Tell me I'm being silly, Steve, that I'm all upset and worked up."

"Of course, you are. We both are. We're talking like a couple of idiots. We have the money. We'll pay it and get our boys back again. And Glenn will take care of his brother."

For a long time they stood, with their arms around each other.

Finally Mrs. Kirtland said, "I've thought of someone."

"What do you mean?"

"Someone else who would have been on the school bus.

It's the girl from that new family, the one that is renting the Busbys' house while they are in Hawaii. I don't know their name, but I do have the Busbys' number."

"Let's phone them now," her husband said.

"No, Jesse did not go to school today," Mrs. French said carefully. "You say your name is Kirtland? Why are you calling me, Mr. Kirtland, and why do you want to know about my daughter?"

"I'm a neighbor of yours," Steve Kirtland told her. "My wife tells me that your daughter attends high school with our sons, Glenn and Bruce." He hesitated.

"Did they go to school today?"

"No, they didn't."

"I see." Mrs. French had been standing, but now her legs felt suddenly too weak to support her. She moved around to the far side of the telephone table and sank into a chair. "And so," she said softly, "it is not just Jesse."

"It's Jesse and our boys and Marianne Paget. There may even be more of them."

"Have you called the police, Mr. Kirtland?"

"No," Steve told her. "We have been afraid to. We are fortunate enough to have money available to pay the ransom. We decided to do that, rather than put the boys into any further danger. Have you called them?"

"I haven't done anything. I haven't known what to do. My husband is away on special duty. In order to get hold of him, I would have to give a reason, and I haven't known what to say."

"You mean, you're alone there?" Steve Kirtland asked incredulously.

"Completely alone. I've been going crazy. It's my fault,

all of it. I was the one who insisted we move to Valley Gardens. I thought it would be good for Jesse, that being part of a settled neighborhood like this would draw her out of her shell a little. But it hasn't made any difference. And if we weren't living here now, she would never have been taken.''

"You can't know that," Steve Kirtland said. "You can't blame yourself for something this crazy. If it could happen this way, out of the blue, it could happen anywhere. The only important thing is getting the kids home again."

"The other people you mentioned," said Mrs. French, "the ones with the daughter, are they paying the ransom? Do they have the money?"

"They are trying to get it. When I last talked to them, they were calling Jack Paget, Marianne's father. He is living in California now and has lots of connections. He always seems to be able to borrow." He paused. "Are you going to be able to pay it?"

"I don't see how—not that much, anyway. We do own some shares in a mutual fund that we were going to use for Jesse's college. I can sell them, but it will take days to do it, and even then I won't have fifteen thousand."

"Maybe we can help you," Steve Kirtland said slowly. "We have a mortgage on the house. We can do some refinancing. Go ahead and get what you can for your mutual fund, and I'll see if I can't manage to make up the difference."

"You would do that—for me!" Mrs. French exclaimed in bewilderment. "But why? I mean, you've never even met me!"

"I know what has happened. I know how you are feeling. Meeting you doesn't have much to do with it. Actually," he continued honestly, "the offer is a selfish one. I think this kidnapping is a package thing. They are not going to release one person and keep the others. They will let them all go at once—or not at all.'' His voice cracked suddenly, as though it were Bruce's. ''We have to have the money! We all have to come through with the money! There can't be any holdouts!''

Mark Crete had his breakfast at eleven thirty. His head ached, and his eyes were bleary. He rinsed the dishes and stacked them in the sink. Then he went upstairs and packed his suitcase.

He left a note for Dexter on the kitchen table:

> Dex—
> Sorry to have missed you this morning—I meant to be up before you left for school, but last night caught up with me. The L.A. trip came through, and I'm off for the weekend. You can reach me at the Alabaster Hotel in an emergency.
> I'm taking a cab to the airport and will leave you the keys to the Jaguar. Will be in Monday evening, TWA Flight 132 if you want to meet it.
> Take care of things, and have a ball!
> Uncle Mark

Then he flipped the switch on the telephone and called his office.

The cab arrived at one twenty. He was just climbing into it when he heard the telephone ringing. It was a muffled buzz from the interior of the house, and Mark hesitated, wondering if he should go back to answer it.

"Oh, to heck with it," he murmured irritably. "I don't

have the time for it. It can't be anything very important anyway."

He settled himself and pulled the car door shut behind him.

"To the airport, please," he told the driver.

The cab swung out of Valley Gardens onto the highway. For a long time the telephone continued ringing.

Chapter Eight

"It's the not knowing," Marianne whispered. "That's the hard part, the not knowing. I wish we were out there with them, where at least we'd know what was going on."

"I wish it were all over and we were away from here and gone." Jesse's face was a pale blur, its expression indistinguishable in the shadows of the bunk room. Through the half-open door they had a partial view of the living room, lit dimly by the fading glow of the dying fire.

"What time is it now?" Jesse asked for what surely was the hundredth time, and Marianne, checking the tiny luminous dial of her wristwatch, said, "It's a quarter past four. They've been out there twenty minutes now. If they were able to get the car started, wouldn't you think they would have done it by now?"

It had been a long night. To Marianne, it seemed a million years since the first step of the plan had been put into effect and she and Jesse had pilfered the key to the storeroom.

Actually Jesse had done it. That in itself had been amazing; that it would be Jesse, moving softly on stockinged feet, who would slip into the second bedroom and search for the key, while in the living room Marianne tried to hold Rita in stilted conversation.

But the past day had brought a change in Jesse. It had been apparent from the moment Friday morning when she had come out to join them by the fireplace and had sent Glenn in to Dexter.

"They killed him," she had told them quietly. "They didn't just tie him up and leave him someplace; they killed him." It was as though the act of speaking the words had released her suddenly from the panic that had bound her. Her chin had steadied; her voice had taken on a note of determination. "We're going to find a way to escape."

"They killed him." Bruce had repeated the statement blankly. "Whom did they kill? What are you talking about?"

"Mr. Godfrey." Marianne had not needed any explanation. "Mr. Godfrey, our driver." For a moment she was too stunned to ask anything further.

"I heard them talking," Jesse continued, "last night. I hadn't wanted to tell you. Until I talked to Dexter, the whole thing seemed so . . . hopeless."

"The poor guy!" There was a break in Bruce's voice. "He was so nice. So darned nice! Why did they do it? They didn't have to!"

"It was probably easier than having to keep him locked up someplace," Marianne said tersely. She tried to divorce her mind from her horror, to see the situation in its entirety, unclouded by emotion. "They committed murder, and it doesn't even bother them."

"It bothers Rita," said Jesse. "I don't think she's as

hard as the other two. I heard her when Buck told her, and she was upset. She said she wouldn't have got mixed up in it at all if she had thought this was going to happen.''

"Who did it?" Bruce asked. "Juan?"

"Yes, but Buck didn't try to stop him. You can see now why we have to get away from here. We can't wait for our parents to pay them.''

"You're right," Marianne agreed softly. "There's no reason now for their letting us go after they get the money. Why should they take the risk of our being able to identify them? They have already killed one person. There is nothing for them to lose by killing five more.''

"Oh, my gosh!" Bruce said weakly. His eyes were wide behind his glasses. "You don't think . . . they wouldn't—I mean, Buck acts almost friendly sometimes.''

"We'll escape," Jesse told him reassuringly. "We will, Bruce. We have to.''

"If anybody can find a way, Glenn can." The use of his brother's name seemed to steady the boy. "Glenn will get us out of here.''

"Of course, he will," Marianne agreed.

But to her surprise it had been not Glenn but Dexter who had organized the escape plan. It was he who had drawn the girls aside to ask about the key.

"Do you think you can get your hands on it? Do you have any idea where Rita keeps it?''

"She took it out of her purse when she unlocked the door for me to bring you coffee." Marianne frowned thoughtfully. "Come to think of it, that's the only time I've seen her with a purse since we've been here.''

"She keeps it in the bedroom," said Jesse, "the one she and Buck share. I saw her carry it in there after.'' She paused and then added slowly, "I could get it if there were some way of keeping them diverted while I was in there."

"There's no sense trying," Marianne said, "until after they have locked the boys in for the night. Then, if I could draw their attention to another part of the house and you slipped in and out quickly, we just might be able to do it."

There had been no opportunity on Friday. Buck and Rita had retired to their bedroom soon after eating, and the angry hum of their arguing voices had gone on and on far into the late hours of the night.

On Saturday, however, the chance had been there. Incredibly it was easier than they had even dared anticipate, for immediately after locking the storeroom door, Buck had left the cabin and driven off in the station wagon, leaving Rita encamped with her inevitable paperback on the sagging sofa in the living room.

"Where has he gone?" Marianne asked her.

"To the village."

"Why?"

"To phone Juan." Rita was not a pretty woman. Her heavy black brows hung low over her eyes, and there was a shadow of a mustache on her upper lip. She regarded the blond girl coldly. "He's already told you that Juan's the one keeping in touch with your folks."

"Why are you doing this?" Marianne asked her. "Is it just for the money?"

"Sure, for money. Why else?"

"There are other ways of getting money." Marianne had been standing at the foot of the sofa, and now she moved closer, seating herself upon the overstuffed arm, swinging her feet so that they brushed back and forth in an irritating rhythm against the roughhewn boards of the floor.

Beyond the arch of firelight she could see Jesse slip silently along the far wall and go into the bedroom.

"I have worked for it." There was bitterness in Rita's voice. "All my life I've worked. You little rich girls don't know what working is. When I was ten years old, I was scrubbing floors in other people's houses. I was the oldest of seven children. Sometimes my earnings were all we had to eat on."

Marianne was shocked, despite herself. "What about your father? Didn't he support you?"

"He was too busy drinking to support anybody. My mother was sick as long as I can remember. She died when I was twelve. After that I had to take all the care of the young ones."

"How terrible!" Marianne kept her eyes glued to the woman's face, willing this spark of communication to hold between them. "Weren't you able to go to school?"

"Not past fifth grade. I read good, though. I've always liked reading. Movie magazines and all sorts of things." She paused and then said, "I met Buck a year ago. He was a repairman. He came to fix the dishwasher in one of the houses where I was working. He asked me out, and we started seeing each other—well, pretty soon we got married. I guess you think that's funny, don't you? A handsome man like Buck marrying a person like me?"

"No. No, it's not funny." Marianne stumbled for words. She kept swinging her feet, scraping them up and down with a grating noise, hoping they would drown out any sound that Jesse might make in the bedroom.

"What are you making all that racket for?" Rita asked her irritably. "Can't you keep your feet still?"

"I'm . . . sort of nervous." Marianne stopped the swinging. "I've never been kidnapped before."

"I've never been part of nothing like this before either."
Rita drew a deep breath. "It's not my idea of fun, and
that's for sure. If it wasn't for Buck . . ."

"Yes?" Marianne prompted.

"You wouldn't understand. You've never lived like I
have."

"I could try to understand," Marianne said encouragingly.

She thought, Jesse, Jesse, what is taking you so long?
For heaven's sake, hurry; I can't keep this going much
longer!

"When a man is as handsome as Buck," Rita said, "a
woman doesn't hold him easy. If a woman didn't go along
with his plans and things, he'd just up and leave her. He's
all I've got, Buck is." She paused. "Can you understand
that at all?"

"Yes, of course," Marianne told her.

Jesse, she thought, please, hurry!

"I might not agree with everything he does. I mean,
they might not be the things I would pick out to do myself.
But when you're married to a man like Buck, you don't
have a choice. Not if you want to hold on to him." She
regarded the girl earnestly. "Can you see that?"

"Yes."

Suddenly, to Marianne's relief, Jesse's slim figure appeared in the bedroom doorway. She stood there for an
instant and then began to move quietly along the wall
toward the open door of their bunk room.

"Yes," Marianne said, "I see."

"It's not like I . . ." Rita paused. "What are you
looking at?"

"What?" Marianne hurriedly focused her full attention
on the woman on the sofa. "What do you mean?"

"You weren't listening to me. You were watching

something." She glared at Marianne suspiciously. Then suddenly she turned to look over her shoulder. "What was it? What were you looking at?"

"Nothing," Marianne insisted frantically, bracing herself for the furor which would surely come. But Jesse had reached the bunk room door and, at the instant of Rita's turning, had slipped inside. The danger of detection was over.

"Mission accomplished!" she announced later when Marianne joined her at last in the bunk room. "It was in her purse, just as I thought, and the purse was on her bed." With a gesture of triumph she held up the key.

"Thank goodness it didn't take you a minute longer." Marianne seated herself on her own bunk. "Now I guess there's nothing to do but wait until Buck comes back. We can't let the boys out of the storeroom until the two of them are asleep."

It had been a long wait. Lying quietly on their bunks, the girls had listened impatiently for the sounds indicating Buck's return from the village. When they came, it was so late that Rita, too, sounded worn-out from waiting.

"What took you so long? I was scared something had happened to you." There was a sharp edge to her voice.

"Nothing happened. I stopped for a few beers."

"You stopped for beers! When you knew I was sitting here going crazy worrying about you? What if the police had got you?"

"How could they?" Buck sounded relaxed and unworried. "There's nothing to connect me with anything. It's Juan who's talked to the kids' parents."

"What's happening?" Rita asked him. "Has Juan made arrangements for the money?"

"Not completely. The Kirtlands and the Frenches have

92

it. The Donavans are trying to get it. He can't get hold of the Crete guy. There's never any answer at the house, and he wasn't at his office.''

"What is he going to do then? Get the money from the two families who have it?''

"Hell, no. We'll have to pick up the whole bundle at once. It's too risky doing it piecemeal.'' There was a creaking of springs as Buck lowered himself onto the aging sofa. "The Donavans—they're the blond girl's folks—are trying to get hold of the girl's father. He's out on the Coast somewhere. They've left messages for him at all his haunts, but he won't answer any of them. Seems like he's the one with the money or the connections to get it, but he has washed his hands of the family and doesn't want to be hauled into their problems.''

In the darkness of the bunk room Marianne stiffened. What was he saying? Perhaps she was not hearing correctly. Buck could not possibly be talking about her father!

"What if they don't reach him?'' Rita asked. "Or if they do and he won't come through with the cash? What if Juan never gets hold of Mr. Crete? Do we settle for the thirty thousand from the other two families?''

"Are you crazy!'' Buck exclaimed contemptuously. "Thirty thousand, after all this risk? Remember, we're going to have to split it with Juan.''

"But how—''

"Look, Rita, when I originated this thing, there were six families involved. That was going to net us a cool ninety thousand. It was a bad break not having the Miller and Lindley kids on the bus. That knocked a third off the winnings right there. No matter what happens, I'm not going to settle for less than sixty. The Donavans have to come through with their fifteen thousand if it means they have to rob a bank to get it. And if we can't reach Crete, the other families will have to make up the difference."

"I don't like this." Rita's voice was so low that Marianne had to strain to make out the words. "I wish we had never got into it."

"You won't wish that when it's over with and we're living high on the hog for a change. You won't say no to a fur coat and a new car and a big house with servants to clean it for you, will you?"

"No." Her voice was still low. "No, I guess not."

"Better dump some wood on the fire before we turn in. It's going to be a cold night."

There was movement in the living room, and after a few minutes there was the sound of Buck going into the kitchen to check the lock on the storeroom door.

"Those boys will freeze in there tonight," Rita commented, and Buck answered, "They'll make it all right. They've got sleeping bags." His footsteps sounded on the wooden floor as he came to stand momentarily in the open doorway to the bunk room. His broad shoulders blotted out the light from the living room, and Marianne lay very still, forcing herself to breathe slowly and deeply. In the bunk across from her Jesse was doing the same.

"They been causing you any trouble?" he asked Rita, and she said, "No. They're scared. They do whatever I tell them to."

"Come on then, let's hit the sack." His voice slurred a little, whether from weariness or the beer he had been drinking, Marianne did not know. He moved away from the door, and for a moment the room lightened and then went into real blackness as he flicked the switch on the living room light.

It had been a few moments before their eyes adjusted

enough to distinguish the soft glow of the fire as it shone through the bunk room door. By that time Buck and Rita had retired to their own bedroom and the house had settled to the silence of the night.

And now there must be more waiting until it was certain that the couple were solidly and permanently asleep. Marianne lay tensely in the heavy quiet, hearing the words that Buck had spoken, the terrible, unbelievable words, uttered so casually in answer to Rita's question: *They've left messages for him at all his haunts, but he won't answer any of them. Seems like he has . . . washed his hands of the family and doesn't want to be hauled into their problems.*

Not Daddy! He can't mean Daddy!

She closed her eyes and he came to her, as he had so many times before, her big, handsome father with his easy charm and his booming laugh.

"Where is everybody?" he would roar, banging the door closed behind him. "I'm home. Where is everybody!" She could remember the rough feel of his jacket against her cheek as he hugged her, the familiar mannish smell of shaving lotion and tobacco. "Where is everybody! Come and welcome your lord and master!"

"We're all here, Jack," her mother would say. She would appear from the kitchen, where she had been doing the dinner dishes, or call down from upstairs, where she was putting the boys to bed. "Where have you been? I kept dinner waiting as long as I could."

"Ran into some old friends. You know how it is." His hand would ruffle Marianne's curls in a careless gesture, as though he were stroking a puppy. "How are you doing, baby? How's my little doll? You're not mad at your old daddy for being late, are you?"

There were times, of course, when he was more than

late, when he never got home at all. There were times when he was away on business trips or visiting some of his many friends or sometimes just wandering.

The time Jay had scarlet fever, he had been gone.

"Where can we get in touch with him?" the doctor had asked, and their mother, her small face pinched with weariness and worry, had answered, "I don't know. I haven't heard from him in over a week now. I don't know how to reach him."

By the time he returned, days later, the crisis had been over.

"I don't see anything to make such a fuss about!" he had exclaimed in apparent bewilderment. "Jay is on the upgrade now, and there's nothing I could have done if I had been here that you weren't already doing." He had paused, and then, when his wife did not answer, he had gone over to her and tilted her face upward and smiled down at her, with the easy affection which was so much a part of his nature. "Hey, honey," he had said softly, "let's have a little smile. Come on, just a little one. Aren't you glad to see me?"

Had her mother smiled? Marianne could not remember. She had not really noticed; she had been too busy watching her father.

"Marianne?"

Startled, Marianne turned in the darkness as Jesse's whisper reached out to bridge the space between them.

"Everything's been quiet for a long time now. Don't you think we had better get started?"

"I suppose we should." Shoving the thoughts of her family from her, Marianne sat up and swung her legs over the side of the bunk. It was a relief to be moving, to be doing something. "Come on," she whispered. "The first thing to do is to get the boys."

It was a simple thing to unlock the storeroom door. The cold of the tiny room came sweeping out to meet them. The boys, fully awake, wrestled their way out of their sleeping bags and came trooping out quietly into the dim warmth of the kitchen.

"What took so long?" Glenn's voice was low. "We were afraid you weren't able to get the key. We had almost given up on you."

"We had to wait until Buck and Rita went to sleep. They stayed up forever." Marianne moved to stand beside him, steadied as Bruce was by the mere fact of Glenn's presence.

Across the kitchen Dexter's glance found Jesse. "You're all right? There has been no trouble?"

"No." Her face was a blur in the shadows. "What's the plan now? Do we all go out to the car?"

"You girls go back to the bunk room." Glenn took over the instructions. "Lie down on the bunks, as though you were sleeping, so if Buck and Rita should happen to waken and look in on you, everything would seem normal. Dex and I will go out and try to get the car started. Bruce will be go-between. When we get the engine going, we'll send him back to get you."

"It will be freezing out there. Wait a minute." Jesse slipped away, and a moment later was back with a heavy leather jacket. She held it out to Bruce. "It's Buck's. He dropped it over a chair in the living room when he came back tonight. You'll need it most. You're the one who will be running back and forth between the car and the cabin."

"Thanks, Jesse." Bruce's hands, as he reached for the jacket, were shaking. Watching him, Marianne thought, he is scared. We are all scared, all except Glenn. Glenn is never scared of anything.

As though in confirmation of her thoughts, Glenn turned to look down at her. "Don't worry," he told her. "In a few minutes now we'll be out of here and on our way home again."

"Good luck," Marianne whispered.

That had been almost half an hour ago.

"They haven't been able to do it." She spoke softly in the darkness of the bunk room. "If they had, they would surely have done so by now."

"At least they are still trying. If they thought it was impossible, they would have given up and come back in." Jesse's voice dropped suddenly to a barely distinguishable whisper. "What was that?"

"What?" Marianne stiffened. Her breath caught sharply in her throat, "Oh, my Lord, somebody is up! Someone is out in the living room!"

"Perhaps it's Bruce?" Jesse breathed hopefully and then said, "No," as a heavy tread moved past their doorway and into the kitchen, and there was the unmistakable sound of a cabinet door being opened, slammed, and reopened.

"It's Buck!" Marianne sat up quickly. "We'll have to go out there!"

"Why? Maybe he's just getting a drink. If we wait quietly, he'll go back to bed again."

"But what if the boys come back in the meantime? They won't know he is up—he hasn't turned any lights on."

She swung herself off the bunk and started out into the living room, conscious an instant later that Jesse was right behind her. Through the kitchen doorway she could see the bulk of Buck's broad shoulders bent forward over the counter, and then, as he straightened and turned, she saw that he had been opening a can of beer.

"What the . . ." He started as he caught sight of the girls. "What are you doing, sneaking around out here? Do you want to get locked in with your boyfriends?"

"We're not sneaking." Marianne tried to make her voice indignant. "We just came out for—for—a glass of water."

"Well, you get back in that bunk room. You can get water in the morning."

He left the kitchen and came through the door into the living room, carrying the beer can with him. He had evidently been asleep, for his red hair was mussed forward over his forehead, and his face had a slack look about it, as though he were still only partly awake. He was fully dressed—of course, we are also, thought Marianne inanely, I guess you don't take time for all the little niceties of life when you're involved in a kidnapping—and she could make out the bulge of the pistol in his trouser pocket.

"We couldn't sleep," she said, "we—"

It was Jesse, standing behind her, who was first conscious of the front door opening. She turned and flung herself backward, as though to block with her slender body the thing that was happening. But her movement was too late, for before she could reach it, the door had swung fully open, and Bruce, impossibly small in the black leather jacket, was framed before them.

"Dex started it!" he said. "He—"

His eyes flicked past them and focused on Buck, and for an instant he stood frozen. The red-haired man was equally startled. For a second all motion hung suspended, and Marianne was conscious of the picture before her, as though it were a painting; the boy in the doorway, his lips still parted with the words he had been about to utter, the fairy-tale scene behind him of snow and trees and the station wagon, its roaring engine throwing up a cloud of steam into the night. And bent over the open hood of the car, clearly outlined in the moonlight, the figures of Glenn and Dexter.

For only an instant it hung there—and then the silence was shattered.

"Run!" Jesse's voice rang out shrilly through the quiet. "Bruce, run! Dex—Glenn—"

Like a startled rabbit, loosed suddenly from captivity, Bruce whirled and bolted, running toward the trees and the roadway beyond. The boys by the car turned also and then, as though suddenly realizing the situation, began to run across the path of moonlight to the protective darkness of the nearest trees.

The taller figure immediately outdistanced the other, and Jesse's voice rang out again, in shriek after shriek, of agonized terror.

"Run! Dexter, run! Hurry! Hurry!"

But the red-haired man had come to life and, shoving past the girls, was running also, his hand reaching for his pocket. A pistol shot rang out across the night, and one of the running figures crumpled and fell.

Marianne opened her mouth to scream, but no sound came.

Chapter Nine

The body of Peter Godfrey, the driver of the missing school bus, was found late Friday afternoon by two little boys who were chasing the family cow. It took awhile for the police to piece together the complete story, for the boys were Mexican and in the excitement of the moment their grasp of the English language deserted them. Their father, to whom they had reported the discovery, was even more agitated, and the result was that it took most of an hour for them to convey the simple fact that a man, with most of his face blown away, was lying in the bushes just west of their farm.

Later that evening an engaged couple, searching for a romantic parking area along the bank of the Rio Grande, discovered and reported the deserted school bus.

Both stories appeared in the Saturday morning paper, along with a photograph of Mr. Godfrey, taken eight years before as a gift for his wife on their twenty-fifth wedding anniversary. A quote from Mrs. Godfrey said, "It is terrible,

terrible. I can't believe it. I can't imagine why anyone would do such a thing. Peter didn't have an enemy in this world.''

Interviews with some of the high school students who had ridden the bus on Thursday afternoon had belatedly brought to light the fact that Mr. Godfrey had not been the driver on this occasion.

"There was a substitute," a sophomore girl was reported as saying. "He was young and kind of cute-looking with red hair and broad shoulders. My girl friend and I kept talking about what a doll he was."

A freshman boy contributed the fact that the new driver had not known the route well, and that he himself had been dropped off on the far side of his regular stop and had been forced to walk back half a block.

"After that," another boy reported, "Bruce Kirtland sat up front with the driver and told him where the stops were."

When the sheriff's officer attempted to follow this track to an ultimate conclusion, Steve Kirtland told them, "I'm sorry, Bruce isn't here right now. I don't know how I can put you in touch with him. Both he and his brother Glenn have taken off on a weekend camping trip."

His hand was shaking when he replaced the receiver on the hook and turned to his wife. "I shouldn't have lied. I should have told them."

"No!" Mrs. Kirtland shook her head violently. "No, Steve. You did the right thing! If word ever gets out that we told the police, we'll never get the boys back again! People who will do something like this won't stop at anything!"

"Murder! Somehow I never thought . . . I guess I didn't want to let myself think . . ."

"The only safe thing to do," Mrs. Kirtland said, "is to give them the money just as soon as possible. We have the full amount. We have to get it to them."

"It's not going to work that way," Steve Kirtland said wearily. "They, whoever they are, aren't going to flit around picking up money here and money there, releasing one kid and then another. That would be crazy. Picking up the ransom is the biggest risk they will be taking, and they will be doing it only once. All the cash has got to be together in one place."

Mrs. Kirtland stared at him, uncomprehending. "But if we have our share of the ransom ready, surely our boys—"

"No, dear," Steve Kirtland said patiently. "That is what I am trying to get across to you. Our boys will be held with the others until the total ransom is collected—from us, from the Frenches, from the Donavans. And from any other family involved."

"But the Donavans don't have their part of it!" Mrs. Kirtland exclaimed. "I talked to Marian just a few minutes ago. She finally reached Jack in California, and he isn't going to contribute one penny."

"He isn't!" Mr. Kirtland exploded. "Good Lord, what's the matter with the man? Marianne is his own daughter! Didn't Marian explain to him—"

"He wouldn't listen to her. The minute she said the word 'money,' he wouldn't let her go any further. He said he would discuss money only through his lawyer and not to call him about it again and banged down the receiver."

"Good Lord," Steve Kirtland said again. He rubbed his hand worriedly across his forehead. "I was sure Jack would come through. I've never thought much of the guy personally, but on something like this, when it's his

103

own kid involved, it never occurred to me he wouldn't cooperate.''

"Can't we help them?" asked Mrs. Kirtland. "For our own boys' sake, can't we make up the difference?''

"We are already doing that for the Frenches," her husband told her. "Even the deepest well runs dry eventually. I've hit every resource we have already. We simply don't have access to anything more.''

The first thing Mrs. French saw when she opened the morning paper was the photograph of Peter Godfrey. It was there, facing her, balanced on the crease, before she ever got the paper unfolded far enough to be able to read the headline. It flashed through her mind that he was a pleasant-looking man, bearing a slight resemblance to a cousin of hers in Ohio, and that he had probably been elected president of some local civic group.

Then she read the name beneath the picture and saw the long black banner stretched across the top of the page: SCHOOL BUS DRIVER FOUND MURDERED.

I don't believe it, Mrs. French thought numbly. It cannot be true.

She closed her eyes and opened them, and the banner was still there. With a violent effort she forced herself to read the article beneath it.

When she finished, she sat quietly with the paper still in front of her. She thought, I very well may never see my daughter again.

The room was empty and very quiet. The only sound was the ticking of the small Swiss clock over the mantel. It was the Frenches' clock; most of the rest of the furnishings in the house belonged to its owners, but it had been Jesse who found the clock in a little shop in Lucerne, Switzerland.

"Look," she had cried, "only sixty francs! Isn't it beautiful?" Her quiet face had been alight with the joy of her discovery. "You had better like it, Mother, for I am going to buy it, and you are going to get it for Christmas!"

Jesse had liked Switzerland. She had liked France. She had liked, Mrs. French thought now, every place she had ever been. For happiness, to Jesse, was not people and activity. It was a self-made thing, deep within herself.

This was something that her gregarious mother had never been able to accept or understand.

"What did you do all day?" she would ask, on her own return from some organized activity, and Jesse would answer, "I read," or, "I walked," or, in Paris, "I went to the Louvre" or "the Bois de Boulogne" or "the Luxembourg Gardens."

"Alone?" her mother would ask, and Jesse would say, "Of course," surprised at the question. "Of course, alone."

"But what about Major Macomber's daughter, that attractive girl we met at dinner the other night? And her brother. Wasn't his name Mike? I'm sure they would have been glad to go with you."

"I just didn't think about asking them," Jesse said casually.

"I worry about her," Mrs. French had said later to her husband. "It's just not natural, her being alone so much or with us and our older friends. She should be frisking around, being a normal teen-ager with youngsters her own age."

"She seems happy," Colonel French had commentd

"Well, possibly she is now, but what about later? How is she going to have a normal social life if she doesn't have any association with her own age-group? Do you realize that Jesse has never even had a boyfriend? By the time I was her age, I had been in love a dozen times already."

"Don't worry so much," Colonel French had said, laughing. "Jesse isn't like you, and she never will be. She'll fall in love, all right, when she's ready to. And when she does decide to share herself with somebody, she is going to have an awful lot to give him."

Jesse, reading—serious, intent, dark hair falling smooth across her cheek . . .

Jesse, on skis—a slim, bright-clad figure, her face lifted to the sun . . .

Jesse, dreaming—Jesse, laughing—Jesse saying gently, as an adult pacifying the whim of a beloved child, "Why, yes. Yes, of course, Daddy. If it will make Mother happy, I'd be glad to live in Valley Gardens."

Jesse—Jesse—Jesse . . .

Mrs. French sat alone in the quiet living room, the newspaper open on her lap. Her eyes were on the clock, not seeing the hands, concentrating instead on the slow, rhythmic swing of the pendulum.

It is not true. It can't be true. Nothing like this could possibly happen to Jesse.

Mark Crete was wakened at ten thirty by the hotel maid, who came in to change the towels in the bathroom.

"Of all fool things!" Mark groaned pitifully. "It's as bad as the nurses in hospitals who come in to take your temperature at the crack of dawn every morning!"

He shut his eyes again with the momentary hope of returning to sleep, but the clatter of cleaning equipment in the hallway outside his door shattered this possibility.

"Oh, well." Mark sighed resignedly and reopened his eyes, hauling himself to a semisitting position. He fished a cigarette out of the pack that lay on his bedside table, lit it, and leaned back against the pillows to think about getting up.

To Mark, business and pleasure trips were one and the same, and every trip he took sufficed for both. His Friday night in Los Angeles had been spent nightclubbing; Saturday morning had been planned for sleeping, and the rest of Saturday, until far into the evening, would be a series of meetings and business discussions of great financial importance both to Mark and to the electronics firm which he represented. At these meetings he would be serious, knowledgeable, and completely dependable.

It was these two things, frolic and business, that made up the life of Mark Crete, with no middle road of domesticity. The only element of family life in his whole bachelor existence was the breakfasts and occasional off evenings that he spent with Dexter.

Now, drawing on his cigarette, he thought about his nephew, as he had found himself doing lately, at odd moments, with a nagging sense of inadequacy. He wished he had seen the boy or at least talked to him before taking off like this for the weekend. Actually, when you came right down to it, he had not seen him since Thursday morning, when the two of them ate pancakes and grunted at each other over separate sections of the morning paper and took off in their separate directions with a minimum of conversation.

I'm not giving the kid much family life, Mark thought with a twinge of guilt, but then, I'm not a family-type guy. I'm forty years old, and I can't swing my whole life around to start playing the father role to an eighteen-year-old who would probably resent it like mad if I tried to anyway. Actually we get along pretty well together.

Dex is a nice enough kid, runs his own life, doesn't make any problems.

Mark had had little contact with Dexter during the earlier years of his life. He had had a very real affection for his sister, Dexter's mother, in their childhood, but time, distance, and the difference in their ways of living had prevented them from retaining a closeness in their adult lives. On the few occasions that he was in the New York area, he had stopped to visit with the family. On the first of these Dexter had been two, a husky, round-faced toddler with an amazing shock of dark hair; on the second he had been eight and away at Scout camp.

When, at twelve, the boy had come down with polio, Mark had been deeply concerned and had insisted on taking over the payment of a number of medical bills.

But this was quite different from taking on personal responsibility for a teen-age boy.

It was after the funeral that he had brought up the subject, almost apologetically. "I know it's hard for you to think ahead at a time like this, Dex, but in their wills your parents named me as your guardian. For business reasons I'm not going to be able to stay here in the East for as long as I would like to, and we're going to have to make some kind of plan for your future."

"I'll be going to college," Dexter said. "Dad always meant for me to do that. He set up a fund for it."

"I know; that's all taken care of. But you have another year of high school to complete first, don't you? It's a little late to register, but I could try to get you into one of the good prep schools . . ."

"Thanks, but no, thanks," Dexter said decidedly. "I don't want to live with a bunch of guys on top of me all the time. I'd rather stay on in the apartment and finish up in public school.''

"That's out of the question. You can't live by yourself in New York City.'' On this Mark was definite. ''There must be prep schools that have private rooms rather than dormitories. We'll pick up some of the catalogues.''

Dexter's eyes glinted defiantly. ''I'm nearly eighteen! I don't need anybody looking after me! I haven't needed anybody for a long time now!''

His jaw was set and stubborn; his left hand was gripped into a fist. From his right sleeve his other hand hung limply, giving him a vulnerable, lopsided look, which tore Mark's heart. For an instant there flashed before him the memory of the round-cheeked baby who had toddled to him across the living room of his sister's first, postage-stamp apartment—a baby with two good arms and two good legs and loving parents, cheering him onward.

The boy before him stood, braced for his decision.

"Look''—Mark heard his own voice speaking—''what would you think of coming back to Albuquerque with me? There's a good public high school in the Valley Gardens area.''

"You mean, to live with you? Would there be room for me?''

"There's no problem about that. I've got a real party house—plenty of room—I could put up an army in there if I wanted to.''

Dexter was hesitant. ''Wouldn't I be . . . kind of . . . a drag on you?''

"I won't let you be,'' Mark said honestly. He was more startled by his own impulsive invitation than Dexter was, and he was already beginning to have qualms about it. However, he had made the offer, and there was no withdrawing it.

"I have a bachelor pad," he said, "and I lead a bachelor life. I'm not home a lot—I take trips, I'm out a lot in the evenings. There's a cleaning woman who comes in once a week, but I do my own cooking, and if you live with me, you'll do yours. I'm not offering you a replacement for what you've lost, Dex. . . . I can't be a parent to you—I won't even try. But I loved your mother very much and—well, if you'd rather live with me than go off to school someplace, I'd like to have you."

"Thank you," Dexter said quietly. "I—I'd like that. I won't be any trouble, I promise."

And it had been true.

Dexter had never been trouble. From the moment he entered the house in Valley Gardens, he had lived his own life, quietly and independently, without making demands of any kind. He cooked his own meals, took care of his clothes, moved in and out of the house on errands of his own without causing a ripple in the smooth flow of Mark's existence. Their schedules of activity overlapped in such a way that often days passed without their so much as seeing each other, with Dexter returning from school just as Mark pulled out of the driveway, and being up and out in the morning before his uncle dragged himself into the kitchen to plug in the electric coffeepot and wake up with a cigarette over the morning paper.

We get along fine, Mark thought now, the kid and I. He's happy—at least, I think he's happy. He can look after himself; he told me that back in New York before I ever brought him out here.

Yet for some reason he felt an odd uneasiness. He had felt it all the past evening. He had taken a whirl at the nightclubs, had some drinks, done some partying, yet at odd moments, sometimes right in the middle of watching a floor show, the feeling would flash over him, a strange, unsettling premonition, that something was not as it should be.

It's all in my head, he told himself firmly. It's because I drove off and left that blasted phone ringing without going back to answer it. It started me off wrong. I can't shake thinking about it.

He lay for a moment longer, inhaling on the cigarette, and then said, "Oh, what the heck," and pulled himself to a sitting position. Reaching for the telephone beside the bed, he asked the operator for long distance. When he heard the thin, brisk voice on the wire, he gave his telephone number in Albuquerque.

There was a moment's silence, and then the phone began to ring. It had a faraway, lonely sound. He could imagine Dexter sitting up in bed, rubbing the sleep from his eyes, staggering down the hall to his uncle's room to fumble for the receiver. Or more likely, because of the time difference, he would already be up and dressed, sitting at the kitchen table. Or reading—the kid was a great one for reading.

The phone continued ringing. Finally the operator's voice said, "I'm sorry, sir; your party does not answer. Would you like me to continue trying?"

"What? Oh—no. No, thanks," Mark said to the invisible voice. "I'm going to be going out soon. I'll try it again later."

He replaced the receiver and glanced around for an ashtray in which to stub out the cigarette.

There's nothing to worry about, he told himself sternly. The kid has taken off someplace for the weekend. Maybe he's gone skiing—to Santa Fe, perhaps, or even to Taos. After all, I left him the Jaguar.

The explanation was so logical that relief flowed through him. Of course, that was the answer. Dexter had gone skiing.

With a grunt of satisfaction, he got out of bed and went into the bathroom to take a shower.

Rod Donavan did not go to work on Friday. Because of this, he was not at his desk at the *Journal* when the first news report came in, and he, like the other families, learned about the death of the missing bus driver by reading about it in Saturday's paper.

His first reaction upon doing so was to dispose of the paper before his wife could read it and to plant himself in a chair next to the telephone so that he could monitor incoming calls.

The one for which he waited arrived around the middle of the morning.

"Yes." Rod said, "we have the money, the whole amount. The Kirtlands and the Frenches have their shares also. How is Marianne?"

"There is another family," the now-familiar voice on the other end of the wire informed him. "A Mr. Crete. I have not been able to contact him at all."

"How is Marianne?" Rod persisted. "I want to speak to her."

"You know she is not with me, Mr. Donavan. I have told you that before. Now listen to me—this is important. I have not been able to contact Mr. Crete about his part of the money."

"Mr. Crete?" The meaning behind the man's words

began to penetrate. "You mean there is a fourth party, not just us and the Frenches and Kirtlands?"

"That is what I am telling you. We must have another fifteen thousand. It is for Mr. Crete's nephew."

"What are you telling me this for?" Rod asked him. "I don't know any Mr. Crete. Does he live here in Valley Gardens?"

"Yes, but he does not answer the phone. He has not answered it at all. I have been unable to reach him. I think he must be out of town."

"I can't help that," Rod said shortly. "I have the money to pay for Marianne's release. I want to know where I should bring it."

"That is the problem, Mr. Donavan. You cannot bring one share or even three shares. We must have the money for all the children at once."

"But how do you expect to collect from someone you haven't even spoken to?" Rod exclaimed. "If Crete is out of town, he may not even know his nephew is missing."

"It matters very little to us," the voice told him, "where the money for his nephew comes from. If Mr. Crete is not there to provide it, then someone else may do so. All that matters if that the full amount, for all five children, is delivered to us tomorrow."

"But fifteen thousand more . . ." Rod tightened his grip on the receiver.

"Can you get it?"

"Yes. Yes, I can get it."

"Today?"

"Yes, today. Where shall I bring it, and when?"

"There is a village," the man said, "about two hours away from Albuquerque. It is a small settlement, in the mountains. There is one road leading to it. You are to drive there alone. If anyone follows you, he will be spotted on the road. You are to bring the money—*all* the money—with you.''

"All right," Rod said, "but Marianne had better be there. I'm not handing you one penny until I see her.''

"There is a church. You will go inside. I will meet you there.''

"With Marianne?"

"I will meet you at the church tomorrow at one o'clock, Mr. Donavan. I repeat, you are to come alone. If anyone is with you or follows you, you will never see your daughter again.''

"I'll be there," Rod told him. "Give me directions.''

When he finally replaced the receiver, he raised his eyes to find his wife standing in the doorway.

"I heard," she said softly.

"Yes. Well, it's all right, honey. It's going to be all right.''

He got up from his chair and went over to her. Marian Donavan moved to lean against him. He put his arms around her and said, "You're shivering.''

"I heard what you told him. You said you could get an extra fifteen thousand dollars for someone else's child. Rod, you can't.''

"No, I can't.''

"We don't even have our own share of the money. We can't pay our own.''

"Don't shiver," Rod said softly. "It's all right. It will be all right.''

"You're going to meet him, and you don't have the money. What are you going to do?''

"I don't know," Rod told her. "But at least I will see

him. I will see Marianne. And I will do something. I don't know what it will be, but I will do something.''

His mind moved swiftly to the collection of firearms in the trunk in the basement, the trunk that Jack Paget had not yet bothered to send for, but that sat there, awaiting his instructions, whenever he decided to take up a permanent residence.

I will do something, Rod thought determinedly. And when I go, one of those pistols is going to go with me.

Chapter Ten

To Jesse, the sound of the pistol shot was inevitable, like the ending of a bad movie. It was the thing for which she had been waiting, the climactic finality of terror which she had known, from the very beginning, was to come.

For the others, it had not been so. Cushioned in the comforting stability of their conventional upbringings, the idea of a kidnapping had held for them the unreality of a television drama. She had seen it in their faces and in their reactions. They were startled, upset, confused, each in his own way frightened, but intrigued as well, as they would have been with a well-plotted story in which, for some mysterious reason, they were pinch-hitting as characters.

Glenn with his blustering, Marianne with her bright bravery, Bruce with his small-boy confidence in the indestructibility of his older brother, Dexter with his dramatic escape plans—none of them had a true doubt about the certainty of a happy ending. The ransom would be paid, of course, or escape would be achieved. Tomorrow or the next day or, at any rate, the day after that, they would be home again, sitting at the family dinner table, reciting the details of their exciting adventure.

They were nice people, all of them bright, normal, above-average teen-agers from good backgrounds. They brushed their teeth and said their prayers and made good grades in high school and would go to college and marry and enter various professions. Dreadful things did not happen to people like this.

It was Jesse who knew that they did happen: Jesse, the dreamer, who read European history, read about peasants who rose in violence against the serene and self-satisfied ruling classes; Jesse, the realist, who had stood in the ruins of German ghettos and marked the paths the Jews had taken as they were herded to their execution; Jesse, who had been brought up in the sharp, blunt service life in which husbands who left in the mornings did not always return in the evenings and the pilots of planes that crashed were more often than not one's friends and neighbors and in which widows continued to buy their groceries at the base commissaries.

From her first glimpse of Juan's face behind the gun, Jesse had seen something there that the others had not. Her eyes, shifting to Buck's, had observed the same look reflected there. And in the conversation she had overheard between Buck and Rita, she had found it again: a cool note of determination, devoid of compassion. This was no game, and these men were not the clumsy, clownish villains of television dramas who turned nervous in a crisis and had a secret sentimental weakness for dogs and children.

There would be no breaks for commercials, no carefully contrived happy endings.

LOIS DUNCAN

At the sound of the pistol shot she began to move forward.

"Buck shot him," she said thinly. "He shot Dexter."

"Don't!" Marianne threw out a restraining arm to block her. "Don't try to go out to him, Jesse. Buck will think you are trying to run with the others. He'll shoot you too!"

"He shot Dexter," Jesse repeated numbly. She stood, pressed against Marianne's arm, shivering in the cold from the open doorway. Twenty yards away the figure in the snow was not moving.

"What's happened?" Disheveled and heavy with sleep, Rita emerged from the back bedroom to shuffle across the living room and crowd in behind them. "What's happened? What was that explosion?"

"Your husband shot Dexter," Jesse told her. "He may have killed him."

The terrible meaning of the words came through to her then with a thrust of such sharpness that it was as though it were her own body which the bullet had entered.

"He may have *killed* him!"

With a sudden twist she broke free of Marianne and began to run out across the snow, her own terror deserted in a sense of overwhelming urgency.

A man's voice shouted behind her, and she could hear Marianne crying, "No. Don't. She's only going to him!" and Rita's voice screaming something equally meaningless.

The shot that she half expected did not come. She reached Dexter and dropped to her knees beside him and was no longer conscious of anything else.

He was alive.

Oh, thank God, Jesse thought, thank God for that much.

118

He was breathing hard, deep, dragging breaths, and then he raised his head and she saw that he was conscious.

"Dex!" She reached to touch him. "Where did he hit you?"

"Don't!" He gave a little gasp as her hand brushed his arm, and she jerked away, horrified at what she might have done.

"Is that the place? Is it your arm?"

"My shoulder. Oh, blast it. The car was finally started! We almost made it!"

"Buck woke up," Jesse told him. "He came out to the kitchen. He was there when Bruce came back to get Marianne and me."

"Is Bruce all right? Glenn—"

"They got away. Buck fired only once. Does it hurt terribly? What can I do?"

She leaned closer, helpless, afraid to touch him or even to brush against his clothing, conscious suddenly of the depth of the cold which pressed about them.

"We'll have to get back inside. Do you think you can walk?"

"Sure. I was hit in the shoulder. You don't have to walk on your shoulder blades." He made a movement as though to get up, leaning on his left arm and struggling to get his legs underneath him, and then he sank back again with a little moaning sound. "I don't know what's wrong. I seem to be so weak."

"Here, let me help you. You can lean on me."

"For gosh sake, Jesse, I'm no lightweight. You can't haul me around like a sack of potatoes."

"I'm stronger than I look," Jesse said firmly.

She moved around to his left side and crouched there, bracing her own arms against the ground as the boy gripped her shoulder and began, slowly and painfully, to pull himself to his feet.

They had almost reached a standing position when the flashlight appeared in front of them and Buck said, "You didn't make it, did you?"

When Dexter did not answer, the flashlight drew closer. It rose to shine directly in their faces.

"You thought you were pulling a cute one, didn't you, getting out of the storeroom, revving the car up without the key, taking off on me! What did you think you were, anyway, a bunch of kid wonders? You been reading too many comic books lately?"

Jesse closed her eyes against the blinding brightness. She was shaking with cold. The sound of her own teeth chattering against each other seemed to fill the night.

Dexter's weight increased as he sagged against her.

"Please," she said, "we have to get indoors."

"Indoors, nothing! You were in such a hurry to get out here to your boyfriend, and he sure went to enough trouble to get out of the cabin." There was controlled fury in Buck's voice. "Now you can both sit out for a while and see how you like it."

"Stay out here?" Jesse could not believe he was serious. "But we can't! We'd freeze to death!"

"That's real tough, isn't it? You should have thought about that sooner."

"Please," whispered Jesse.

Dexter moved against her, trying vainly to shift his weight so as not to lean so heavily.

"Jesse didn't do anything," he said weakly. "I'm the one who had the idea about starting the car. I was the one who was running. You don't have to punish her for that."

"It's all one to me," Buck said, "what happens to any of you. All you are to me is your cash value. Fifteen thousand each is what you're bringing, and so help me, you're making me earn every cent of it." Abruptly he lowered the flashlight. "Rita," he called to the woman in the doorway, "you let these two wait out here until I get back. Let them cool their heels for a while, and maybe they'll realize how well-off they were as our guests."

"Where are you going?" Rita sounded worried. "You're not going off someplace—"

"I'm going to chase down those other two. They can't have got too far. There's only one road down, and they're going to have to take it."

"Let them go, Buck," Rita urged him. "They can't get as far as the village in this cold. They'll have to come back to the cabin soon anyway."

"That big kid might make it," Buck muttered. "At least there's a chance of it. We can't afford to take chances."

"What are you going to do?" Rita asked anxiously. "Buck, you promised—it's Juan who does the strong-arm parts. We discussed that in the beginning. You and I are keeping our hands clean of it."

"Well, plans change. We didn't count on something like this happening."

Without further comment Buck turned and crossed the clearing to the station wagon. The motor was still running. We could have been in it, Jesse thought achingly. We could have been halfway down the mountain by this time.

Buck climbed into the vehicle and slammed the door behind him. The sound of the engine rose to a roar as he clamped down on the accelerator. The headlights came on in two glaring beams, reducing the moonlight to diluted darkness.

"We can't let him go!" gasped Jesse, and Dexter said ruefully, "There's not much we can do to keep him from it."

They stood in silence, watching the car as it backed, straightened, and rumbled forward out of the cabin clearing onto the twisted dirt road.

The headlights disappeared behind the thicket, and darkness closed in upon them again. Rita's squat figure filled the width of the cabin doorway.

Marianne's voice was clear and sudden. "You are going to let them come inside, aren't you? They'll freeze out there. Jesse doesn't even have a coat on."

"I can't," Rita told her. "Buck just now said for me not to."

"He couldn't have meant it! He might not be back for hours! People can't stay out in cold like that unless they are dressed for it!"

Jesse, listening, let Marianne do her arguing for her. The cold had settled through her now like a gigantic weight, filling all of her being. She was no longer conscious of shivering, just of a kind of numbness without beginning or ending.

Suddenly Dexter's weight upon her shoulders increased in such measure that she stumbled beneath it, catching herself with a violent effort to keep from falling.

"Oh, no," she exclaimed, "no!"

Her stomach lurched in fear, as she felt his head fall limply to settle upon her shoulder.

"Help me!" she cried. "Please, come help!"

"I'm coming!" Marianne shoved her way past the uncertain woman in the doorway and ran out to them. She reached for Dexter on the other side and slid her arm around him, shifting part of the burden of his weight to her own shoulders.

"Be careful," Jesse warned her frantically. "That's the bad side. That's where Buck shot him."

"Lord, Jesse, he's bleeding like mad! No wonder he's fainted!" With a sound of horror Marianne began to struggle forward. "Come on, start walking. Even if we have to drag him. We've got to get him where we can take care of him."

"But Rita won't . . ." Jesse choked down a sob.

"She'll have to." There was steellike determination in Marianne's voice. "Rita, you've got to let us in. We have to get Dex in where we can stop the bleeding."

The older woman regarded them uncertainly. "You heard Buck. He wants these two outside until he comes back. What will he say if he comes back and I haven't done what he told me?"

"What if he comes back," Marianne asked harshly, "and Dexter's dead? What if he's bled to death out here in the snow?"

"Dead?" Rita eyed the unconscious boy nervously. "He's not dead. You can see, he's breathing."

"Juan is supposed to do the strong-arm parts. I just heard you say it. Juan wasn't the one who shot Dexter. If Dexter dies, it's your husband who'll get the blame for it! It's Buck, not Juan, who will be a murderer!"

Numbly Jesse listened to the words the other girl was speaking. Shot. Dead. Murdered. Fantastic words, yet real—horribly real. He is not going to die, she told herself frantically. It is just a shoulder wound. People don't die from shoulder wounds. It's cold. Oh, Lord, it's cold.

"Buck's all you've got," Marianne was saying. "You

told me yourself. You can't let him do this thing. You can't let him kill somebody.''

"He's going to be mad, he is,'' Rita said hesitantly. "He's going to raise Cain when he gets back.''

But despite the words, she was moving sideways.

She is letting us in, Jesse thought incredulously.

They were moving forward, through the doorway. Warmth flowed out to meet them, blessed warmth, lapping about them.

"This better not be a trick now,'' Rita said cautiously. "He better be really hurt like you say he is.''

But somehow, with the departure of Buck, her voice carried no authority. It was Marianne who, ignoring her, said firmly, "We better get him into the bedroom.''

Wordlessly Jesse followed her directions. Slowly, slowly, a million miles across the living room. A sideways struggle through the narrow bunk room door. Another million miles across the tiny room to the closest bed.

"Let's get him flat. Do you know anything about first aid, Jesse? Oh, my gosh . . .'' Marianne's face went suddenly white. "Look at the blood! The bullet must have severed a vein or something—he's bleeding all over everything!''

"It's not as bad as that. It looks more than it is, I think.'' Jesse eased the boy gently onto the bed, eying the punctured jacket through which the dark liquid was rapidly seeping. "We'll need hot water,'' she said, "and bandages.''

"I'll get them.'' Marianne's assurance seemed to have deserted her. "I've never seen anybody bleed that way.''

"I took a course in first aid once. All the service kids had to take it.'' To her surprise, Jesse found that their positions were suddenly reversed. Now it was she who was steady, she who was issuing directions. "Go get the water and anything we can use for bandages. I'll get the jacket off so we can see exactly how bad a wound it is."

The boy on the bed moaned softly, turning his head to one side. "They never knew . . ."

"What?" Jesse leaned forward, straining to catch the words. "What is it, Dex?"

"They never knew." The boy opened his eyes and said quite clearly, "My parents are dead. They never knew that I loved them."

It was such a strange statement that Jesse stared at him in bewilderment, until she realized that he was still not fully conscious.

"Of course, they did," she said soothingly, hoping that her response was the right one.

"The way I acted. They never knew . . ."

"They knew," said Jesse.

Marianne came back into the room, carrying a bowl of hot water and the torn pieces of a hand towel.

"Is it okay if I don't stay and watch?" she asked nervously.

"I can manage," Jesse assured her.

"That was Marianne, wasn't it?" Dexter seemed clearer now. He started to lift his head, caught his breath, and lowered it again quickly. His eyes were focused. "Where is Buck?"

"He took the car back down the mountain road." Jesse did not tell him the purpose behind the departure. "Can you help me, Dex? I need to get your jacket and shirt off."

"Why?" He looked suddenly suspicious.

"To bandage your shoulder, of course."

"It's all right. It doesn't need to be bandaged."

"But it does!" She regarded him with surprise. "We have to stop the bleeding."

"It's just a nick! I'll take care of it!" There was real panic in his voice. "I'll bandage it myself!"

"You can't reach it, Dexter! At least, let me help you."

"I said, I'll take care of it." He raised his arm in a violent gesture, and gasped as the sudden bolt of pain shot through him. His face drained of color, and for an instant Jesse thought he had fainted again.

"Lie down," she begged, "here. Please!" She pressed him back upon the pillow, and he drew a long, choking breath and closed his eyes.

"Okay," he said weakly.

"I'll be gentle. I'll try not to hurt you."

"It's not that."

This time when she reached for his jacket he did not stop her. He merely lay there resignedly as she undid the buttons and turned obediently on his side while she gently worked the sleeve of first the jacket and then the flannel shirt down from the injured shoulder.

It took a moment for understanding to reach her.

"There," Dexter said softly. "There, now you see. Aren't you glad we don't have to be seen on the beach together?"

Jesse sat in silence, gazing down at the boy before her, at the sturdy man's body with the wasted, underdeveloped arm and shoulder no bigger than a child's.

So this is the reason, she thought. This is the reason for all the anger, the defensiveness, the bitterness. This is the reason for Dexter Barton.

"All right," Dexter muttered coldly, "you've looked long enough now. The second show doesn't start until noon." He paused, and when she did not answer, a tremor came into his voice. "Well, why don't you say something?"

"There is nothing to say," Jesse told him, and she leaned over and kissed him. It was the first time she had done such a thing in her life.

Chapter Eleven

Bruce heard the pistol shot when he had almost reached the trees. The sound lent wings to his feet, and with a final spurt of speed he cleared the last space of moonlight and plunged into the welcoming shadows of the thicket.

Another figure crashed in beside him, and for a moment the two of them clawed their way through the bushes, gasping and struggling, shoving aside branches and fending off the brambles that whipped across their faces, until at last they were clear on the far side with the dirt road curving ahead.

"Blast it!" Bruce heard his brother's voice mutter. "This would have to happen just when we had the engine going and everything set. If Dex hadn't been so stubborn about sending you back to get the girls . . ."

"Dexter!" Bruce grasped at the name, his breath coming in short gasps. "Where is he?"

"I don't know. He started out right behind me."

"The pistol shot! You don't think—"

"Of course not. Buck fired that shot to scare us. He couldn't have taken good aim from the doorway." Glenn had steadied his breathing now and seemed calmer. "Come on, kid, we had better get going."

"Where?" Bruce regarded him blankly. "Where can we go? It's twenty miles to the village."

"We've got to try it. We can't stay here and let Buck catch up with us."

"We've got to wait for Dexter."

"That's crazy." Glenn had already started along the roadway, moving at a dogtrot so that the younger boy was obliged to jog in order to keep up with him. "Dex could never hike this. He's got something wrong with his leg. You know how it buckled just on the ride up here."

"But we can't leave him!" Bruce insisted. "If his leg is bad, he'll need us to help him."

"We can't wait for him."

"But why can't we? If we stand in the shadows, we can see Buck coming . . ."

"Bruce, look." Glenn drew a long breath. "Dex isn't coming. There isn't any sense in waiting for him. He—he went back to the cabin."

"He couldn't have. What reason would he have for doing a fool thing like that?" Bruce fought against the question; then full realization struck him. "He was hit, wasn't he? You told me that he wasn't!"

"I didn't want to have to tell you. Yes, he was hit. I heard him fall."

"Do you think . . . was he . . ."

"I don't know. How can I know? It's just darned sure that we can't go back there. Marianne and Jesse will take care of him. If there is anything to be done, you know that they'll do it. The thing for us to do is to keep on going."

129

He paused and then said, "You know that's right, don't you? We have got to keep going."

Reluctantly Bruce nodded. "Will Buck be following us, do you think?"

"If he does, we'll hear the engine of the station wagon in time to get off the road. I shouldn't think he would try following us on foot. Not in this cold, without his jacket."

Bruce crammed his hands into the leather pockets of Buck's jacket, conscious suddenly of the warmth of the wool lining against his body. He thought of Jesse's bringing it to him and was filled with a surge of gratitude. At the time there had been no way for any of them to know how important the gesture would turn out to be.

The night was cold, but it was a still, windless cold. Bruce could feel it like a dull pressure upon his shoulders and a stinging sensation on his lips and ears. The moonlight, falling in an eerie silver glaze upon the ice-encrusted road, gave the moment a feeling of unreality.

It is as though, Bruce thought, this is something I have dreamed a million times before. Any moment now I may open my eyes and find that I am in my bed at home, dreaming it again.

It it had not been for the circumstances behind the situation, it might have been almost pleasant for him, trotting alongside Glenn, the two of them drawn together by their very existence, as lone human beings, in a world of stillness and snow.

He was not afraid. It was impossible to be afraid with Glenn beside him. There had been times when as a child he had imagined such a moment, the peak of a challenging adventure with Glenn to share it. In these childhood fantasies there had sometimes been tornadoes, sometimes earthquakes, or invading armies from other planets. It had not mattered what the danger was. The important thing had been that it was he and Glenn, banded together, who were combating it.

But never in his wildest imaginings had he envisioned a kidnapping, a blazing pistol, a mountain hideaway. It was as though a dream had suddenly gone out of control and become life-size.

He glanced sideways at his brother, suppressing an urge to reach out and touch him.

And then he heard it: the sound on the road above them. It took them both a second to register what it was.

"That's the engine," Glenn exclaimed. "It's the station wagon! Buck is trying to follow us!"

"We've got to get off the road!"

Bruce glanced around quickly. There was only one direction in which it was possible to turn, for to the left the road fell off in a steep drop-off to the woods below. To the right there rose an embankment and above that the protective shelter of heavy underbrush.

It was toward this that Glenn was already beginning to run.

"Hurry," he shouted, and Bruce, turning to follow, felt his feet slip from under him on the icy smoothness of the road. He struggled to regain his balance, knowing even as he did so that it would not be possible.

He caught himself as he fell, taking the brunt of the impact on his arms and knees. For a moment he scrambled on ice, trying to get his feet beneath him, wishing frantically that he were wearing boots instead of his school shoes. Then he was standing, but the wasted moment was one which should not have been lost.

In that instant the station wagon rounded the curve behind him, and the road was flooded with the glare of headlights.

131

For one frozen second, Bruce stood petrified. Then he began to run.

To run—but where? There was no place to go. There was no time now to follow Glenn up the steep embankment, no time to search for a pathway down the cliff to the left. There was only the road ahead down which to run, a perfect target centered in the glare of the headlights. Like Dexter, Bruce thought, he shot Dexter while he was running, and now he will shoot again, and he cannot miss, not possibly!

But Glenn was safe! That thought sustained him. For some strange reason he thought of Jesse. There was no reason for her to come into his mind then, but she did, flashing briefly across his vision—and then his parents, with their open, loving faces.

The sound of the engine rose to a roar as Buck mashed down upon the accelerator.

Bruce's breath was coming in ragged gasps, and in his ears he could hear his blood pounding in a harsh, wild rhythm. His legs were moving with a speed of which he had not known he was capable.

I will not die, he told himself with vehemence, no matter how often he shoots me. No matter where the bullet hits me, I will not die! I will keep running and running. I cannot die, not yet, not now! There are too many things I have never done!

And strangely it was this last thought, beyond any feeling of fear, which drove him in a final, superhuman burst of effort to round the next curve and stagger into the shadows which lay beyond.

For an instant he was engulfed in darkness, and then the headlights were again upon him, but something was different. They had changed direction! He was no longer centered in the flood of brightness but was on its edge, poised at the intersection of light and darkness. Again he was falling, but this time it was not he who had lost balance but the road itself that was rising in a drunken lurch to meet him.

With a last motion of exhaustion Bruce twisted backward, just in time to see the bulk of the station wagon on the road behind him, moving sideways in a slow arc toward the left side of the road. Shadows leaped wildly as the light slid past him. The wheels of the car were spinning; the engine was roaring.

From his sprawled position, Bruce watched, hypnotized, as the car drifted onward. So slowly it moved that it did not seem possible. It was as though an invisible hand had reached for it and were drawing the vehicle gently, deliberately across the ice to the cliff's edge.

And then—in one incredible instant—beyond it.

There was a ripping sound, a series of thudding crashes as the car struck trees, passed them, struck others below. And then there was silence.

Silence. So total that Bruce, lying quietly in the empty road, could hear the far, faint whisper of pine needles as they bent together under their crusting of snow. He could hear his heart beating and the rasping, labored noise of his own breathing.

For a long time he lay there, unmoving. Then he became conscious of approaching footsteps and of his brother's voice.

"Bruce? Bruce, are you all right?"

Bruce nodded slowly in the darkness.

"Bruce, where are you? Bruce?"

"Yes. Yes. I'm okay." He formed the words carefully, hearing his voice, cracked and distant, as though it were that of a stranger. "I'm here. I'm okay."

"Why didn't you answer when you heard me calling? Lord, kid, I thought he'd got you!"

Glenn had reached him now; Bruce could feel him beside him.

"Are you sure you're all right?"

"He didn't shoot at me."

"Of course, he didn't. He was going to run you down instead! When he slammed on the car brakes . . ."

Bruce nodded weakly. "The car . . ."

"It was coming too fast for this road. It hit that ice and went into a skid."

"He went over . . . the cliff. . . ." Dizziness swept over him; he struggled against it. The world was tilting precariously about him.

"Bruce, what's the matter?" Glenn's voice was very close. "I thought you said you were okay!"

"I am. I just . . ." Nausea struck him in a wave, doubling him over. "The car . . . went over . . ."

The sickness came upon him, tide upon tide of it. Against the black screen of his eyelids the car came skidding, turning, sliding, the headlights sweeping in a long, slow arc. He could see the driver's face. Buck's face, staring through the windshield, the eyes wide with terror, the mouth open in a silent scream at the knowledge of what was happening and could not be controlled. In actuality he had not been able to see into the car, had not seen the driver, but now in this second vision he could see and did see, and the sickness came again and again as the car slid nearer and nearer to the edge, like a child's toy on a tilted tabletop—and then went over.

"Bruce, stop it, do you hear me! Get hold of yourself!" Glenn's voice cut into his consciousness. "Come on, we've got to get moving. You can't keep sitting there in the snow. You'll freeze!''

Slowly the sickness subsided. Bruce opened his eyes. The world looked soft and blurred in the moonlight.

"Get up," Glenn told him, and he did so, finding to his surprise that his legs could hold him. He was no longer shaking.

He felt very calm.

"I guess," he said, "we had better start looking for a way down the cliff to the car."

There was a moment's silence. Then Glenn asked, "Why?"

"To see what we can do to help. He might still be alive in there. There is always a chance. We can't know. . . ."

"You must be crazy," Glenn said incredulously. "It's Buck who was in that car. He was trying to run you down."

"Yes, but—"

"What the devil do you want to go down to him for? What if through some miracle he is alive? What do you think you're going to do about it?"

"It would depend on how badly hurt he was," Bruce said reasonably. "We can't tell until we reach him. If he is alive, surely we can do something."

"Bruce, that man was trying to kill you. That's why he went over the cliff. He was trying to kill you! It's just by luck that you're alive and standing here now. Don't you understand, you don't owe him one blasted thing!"

"You mean . . ." Bruce stared at his brother, not certain he was hearing him correctly. "You think we should leave him there?"

'You're darned right I do. We've got ourselves to think about. We've got a long trek in front of us if we're ever going to make that village. We'd better be getting on with it.''

"You do mean it, don't you?" Now it was Bruce's turn to be incredulous. "You really mean it.''

"Of course." Glenn's handsome face was planes and shadows in the moonlight. "What is Buck to me? What is he to you, for Pete's sake?''

"He is a human being.''

The wall was there between them, thin and invisible, but there, solid, like a sheet of cold glass. It was, Bruce thought miserably, the way it had so often been in their childhood. He was with Glenn, close, an arm's length away, yet somehow he could not touch him. Raising his face, he tried to see into his brother's eyes, but he could not do so. In the dim light they were dark pockets hidden in shadow.

"He is human.'' Bruce struggled to find the words. "He is down there, and maybe—maybe . . . he is alive. If we don't get to him, we'll never know. We'll never be sure. We'll go the rest of our lives not knowing but that we might have been able to save him. I couldn't live with that, Glenn, could you?''

He paused. His brother did not answer.

"Could you?'' Bruce persisted. "Could you live with that and not feel guilty about it every day of your life?''

"Yes,'' said Glenn.

For a long moment neither of them spoke. The silence hung between them, part of the wall, but now, at last, the wall was defined.

Slowly Bruce reached out and touched his brother's arm. "The other night,'' he said, "that car accident. It didn't really happen the way you said it did, did it? Another car didn't hit you. That scrape and dent—they weren't really made by a car at all.''

"Of course, they were," Glenn said carefully.

"You didn't really let your insurance lapse. That isn't the reason you didn't want Dad to know about it. You got the car fixed so fast. The whole thing repainted."

"What are you trying to say?"

"It was Monday that Joan Miller's brother was hit by that hit-and-run driver. It happened less than a mile from our house on Monday night, right there at the entrance to Valley Gardens."

Glenn regarded him blankly. "I don't know what you're talking about."

"Oh, Glenn." Bruce spoke the name softly. "Glenn."

It was the name he had spoken so often in the past, with pride, almost with reverence, the strong, shining name which was his brother's.

"Glenn," he said now, and pain tore through him.

Say that I'm wrong, he begged silently. Oh, Glenn, please, please tell me that I'm wrong!

"It was late," Glenn said. "I was tired. I didn't expect a blasted scooter to be zipping around at that time of night. It was his fault as much as mine. He came shooting out of a side street."

"But you didn't stop," Bruce said shakily.

"There was nothing I could have done, Bruce. Lights were going on in all the houses. I knew that people had heard the sound of the accident and would be taking care of things. It wasn't as though I were leaving him on a side road someplace without calling for help. What would it have accomplished if I had stopped and got out and everything? There would have been a big furor. The folks would have been pulled into it. My license might have been revoked." Bruce's hand was still on his arm. He covered it now with his own. "You can see that, can't you, Brucie?"

His voice was warm and persuasive.

Bruce slid his hand out from under his brother's. He thrust both hands deep into the pockets of Buck's jacket.

"No," he said.

"Oh, now look, kid." Glenn moved as though to put an arm around his shoulders, thought better of it, hesitated. "You're not going to make a big thing out of this, are you, Brucie?"

"A big thing?"

"When we get back, I mean. You could get me in one heck of a lot of trouble. Besides, I'd deny it. You don't have proof of anything."

"No."

"The car is fixed up by now. They can't compare marks or anything. I told the guy at the garage that I scraped it on a fence post. He believed me. Other people will believe me, too. It will be my word against yours. I can even show them the fence post. It's way out on South Ten."

"Don't," Bruce said chokingly. "Don't, Glenn."

"People believe me. You know that. You'll just look like a jealous kid brother, trying to get into the limelight. And if you did convince anybody, what would you be achieving? It wouldn't help the Miller kid any. He'll either get well or he won't, regardless. Our parents would go to pieces. Mother might even have a nervous breakdown."

"Don't," Bruce said again. "I don't want to hear you say these things."

"I'm just trying to show you how it would be."

"I already know."

"Then you're not—" There was relief in Glenn's voice.

"I promised you already. Back last Monday night."

"Sure. Sure, you did. I knew you wouldn't fall down on me. You're a good guy, Brucie."

He reached out to clap the younger boy on the shoulder, and Bruce moved backward, avoiding the touch. He felt very tired.

"You'd better go," he said. "You've got a rough hike ahead of you."

Glenn regarded him with surprise. "Aren't you coming?"

"I'm going to climb down and see about Buck."

"Lord," Glenn said with a touch of grudging admiration, "you're a stubborn kid, aren't you? Well, go ahead then. I'll make it faster without you anyway."

"I'm sure you will."

"Can't you picture the headlines? 'LOCAL FOOTBALL HERO HIKES TO RESCUE!' I'll be famous."

"I'm sure you will," Bruce said again.

The sky was beginning to lighten. In the east a faint glow of pink showed beyond the trees. The trees themselves were starting to take form, no longer dark masses but trunks and branches, black against gray.

In the lessened darkness Bruce could see his brother's face more clearly. He could see his eyes. They were wide and beautiful, and there was no guilt in them.

"Say, look," Glenn said thoughtfully, "this is going to be a long, cold haul. Since you're just going to take a look at the wreck and go back to the cabin, what would you say to letting me take Buck's jacket?"

Chapter Twelve

The church was silver.

It is impossible, Rod Donavan thought, as he drove slowly up the winding mountain road, past the few small stores, the sprinkling of shabby adobe houses, toward the shining structure on the hillside before him. It must be worry, he thought, and the lack of sleep. My mind must be slipping. I'm seeing things. Nobody builds churches out of silver.

And then he drew closer and saw that it was aluminum, a prefab building which might originally have been intended for a storehouse. Somehow the congregation must have acquired the pieces and fitted them together and mounted them with a steeple of some other, more common material, which had been painted white. It was the morning sunlight which had given the construction the illusion of grandeur, glancing off the metal walls with an iridescent brilliance.

An omen, Rod thought hopefully, of what can be accomplished with nothing.

The comparison was too labored to be comforting.

He did not let himself dwell upon the subject. He parked the car at the side of the road, opened the glove compartment, and took out the pistol. Rod, who had never handled a firearm before, had spent twenty minutes working out the mechanics of loading it before he was satisfied that he had this accomplished correctly.

Now he sat, weighing the deadly black object on the palm of his hand, trying to decide upon the best thing to do with it. His first impulse was to slide it into his trouser pocket for the simple reassurance that its presence would give him. It seemed impossible, however, that he could carry it there without detection, for would not a concealed weapon be the first thing that would be looked for by any man, or men, who would be meeting him? And once the weapon had been located and taken from him, he would, for all practical purposes, be rendered as helpless as Marianne herself.

No, it was better to trust to luck for the moment and hope that the pistol could be worked into the situation at some later time when its presence would be more crucial.

He glanced quickly about the interior of the car in search of a hiding place. The glove compartment was too obvious. So was the trash receptacle, with the added disadvantage that its position on the far right of the car would prevent its being reached by anyone in the driver's seat.

His eyes traveled downward, pausing as they reached the torn spot in the upholstery, where the spur of one of Jay's cowboy boots had snagged and caught. Bending forward, Rod investigated the tear. The material was old, and the rip lengthened easily under his fingers. When the hole was large enough, he thrust the pistol in, beneath the cover itself, forcing it back into the springs.

Then, with a sigh of satisfaction, he drew the cloth together again as well as he could, got out of the car, and went into the church.

On first view the building appeared to be completely empty. After the glare of the outside the church interior was dark and quiet. The lack of insulation and the open doorway brought the cold inside, where it lay, layer upon layer, untouched by the thin rays of the winter sun. At the front of the church candles gleamed dimly, and a lone skylight, half-covered with snow, admitted enough light to illuminate the clumsy hand-carved crucifix which hung over the altar.

Straight-backed chairs, shoved out of alignment, gave evidence of the fact that there had been an early service which had been attended by at least a few shivering worshipers.

Drawing his overcoat more tightly around him, Rod glanced at the luminous hands of his watch. It was not yet one. He was early. Marian teased him sometimes about the fact that he was always early for things.

At the thought of his wife, he again saw her face, as he had seen it last, raised to his with a look of entreaty which was almost desperation.

"Rod, I want to come, too! I want to come with you!"

"Marian, no." He had answered her firmly, trying not to let his own emotion show in his voice. "You stay here with the boys. Your coming would accomplish nothing. It would only complicate things."

"No, it wouldn't. You might need me. What will they do when they realize that you don't have the money?" Her eyes were wide and frightened. "They might hurt you!"

"Not in a church, dear. I'm to meet them in a church,

remember? And this is Sunday. There will be people around, a whole congregation."

He had intended the words for comfort, but he had spoken them with sincerity. He had not envisioned a small mission church with its one early-morning service over, as dark and empty as it might have been on a typical weekday.

"Besides, I don't intend to let them know that I don't have the money," he added gently. "Not, at any rate, until they have taken me to Marianne. And after that, well, I am not unarmed. Whatever happens, I have Jack's pistol."

He should not have said this. He saw her face tighten.

"Oh, Rod, you shouldn't be doing this. The police should be going! You've never fired a gun in your life! You must take someone with you. Let's call Steve Kirtland!"

For an instant he was tempted. Then he shook his head. "I told the man on the phone that I would come alone. You heard me tell him. If he sees I have someone with me, he may think I am breaking my word. He may not speak to me at all, and the whole thing will be for nothing."

This argument got through to her. She accepted it grudgingly. "When you talk to him, when you learn anything, you will call me? You'll let me know?"

"As soon as I possibly can, dear."

"You're to meet him at one o'clock. If I don't hear from you by three, I'm calling the police, Rod."

"No, give me longer than that. Say, until five. Let me have four hours."

"Until four. No longer. If I don't hear by four, I will know that something has happened."

She had clung to him hard for a moment, and standing there, his arms about her, Rod was filled, as he often was, with perplexity at the thought of Jack Paget, who could detach himself so completely from all bonds of emotion and walk away and leave his family without a glance behind him.

Now, in the quiet of the church, he drew a slow breath and squared his shoulders.

"I, Rodney, take thee, Marian."

Only a matter of months ago he had spoken these words, but from that moment on they had become a deep and intricate part of him. Rodney Donavan was not a big man or a handsome one; he was not clever or charming or witty or financially successful. He was a slight, balding, near-sighted man with a gentle face, but he had taken his vow solemnly, amending it in his own mind: "I, Rodney, take thee, Marian—thee and thy children and all the problems and joys that go with them—for better and for worse, as long as we all shall live."

The sound of a footstep brought him out of his reverie. Turning, he saw the man in the leather jacket who had moved out of the shadows.

For a moment, Rod was not certain that this was the person for whom he had been waiting. Short, dark, square-set, with a swarthy complexion, he could have been any Mexican villager, stopping in the empty church for a few moments of quiet meditation.

And then he spoke, and Rod's hesitation vanished, for it was the same voice as that on the telephone, soft, accented, terribly familiar.

"You are waiting for someone?"

Slowly Rod nodded. "I'm here for my daughter."

"You have come alone?"

"You can see that I have." Rod kept his voice level. "Where is Marianne?"

"She is all right. You will see her shortly." The man's eyes shifted. "First the money."

"First my daughter," Rod said firmly.

"We do not argue about this, Mr. Donavan. I make the rules here." The man's voice was cold. "The money first, please. You have it with you?"

"First," Rod insisted, "I want to see Marianne."

"I hold the cards here, I think, Mr. Donavan. The girl is more important to you than the money is to me. I can walk out of here now, and you will never see me again. Me or your daughter. I will be losing nothing."

"You will be losing sixty thousand dollars," Rod said quietly.

For a moment they stood, weighing each other, in silence.

The man was frowning. "You have it with you? The entire amount?"

"Every cent of it," Rod lied stolidly.

"You are carrying it now?"

"Of course not. I wouldn't be that foolish. It is locked in the trunk of my car. I have hidden the trunk key. You will never find it without my cooperation. And I won't give it to you until I see my daughter and know that she is all right."

"You are a stubborn man, Mr. Donavan," the Mexican said slowly.

"I am a determined man," Rod told him.

He knew there was a gun. It was not in evidence, but it was there. He was not certain how he knew it, but his consciousness of its presence was a sharp reality in the dreamlike shadows of the quiet church.

He could shoot me, Rod thought. He could shoot me now and take the car keys and go. Later, somehow, he could open the car trunk—pry it, dynamite it, get it open somehow. He does not need me.

There was, however, the fact of those adobe houses. The fact that it was Sunday and people would be home, eating their dinners, playing with their children. The sound of a pistol shot echoing forth from the church could be heard in those houses or by anyone walking or driving along the street outside.

It was a risk, and this man was not going to take risks. Not with sixty thousand dollars.

Rod regarded him squarely. "Will you take me? I will give you the money as soon as I see that Marianne is safe."

The man shifted his shoulders in a shrug. "As you like."

"Let's go then."

They left the church together, moving side by side down the narrow aisle and out into the sunlight. After the darkness the shattering brilliance of the snow-laden world burst upon them with blinding intensity.

Squinting his eyes against the glare, Rod led the way across the road to where his car stood, parked on the siding. He opened the car door, then hesitated.

"Do you want me to drive?"

"One moment, please."

With practiced dexterity, the man reached over and ran his hands down the outside of Rod's jacket, over the chest and pockets, under the armpits. Then down the trousers, over the hips, along the inside of the legs to the ankles.

With a sense of relief Rod silently thanked heaven for the impulse that had made him leave the pistol behind him when he went into the church.

He tried to smile wryly. "Satisfied that I'm not carrying anything?"

"You may get in now. You do the driving. I'll tell you where."

The man came around and got in on the far side, in the seat next to the driver. Rod put the key in the ignition and started the engine. He pulled off the siding onto the road.

"Which way?"

"Straight. I'll tell you where to turn off."

The man leaned back against the seat. His right hand was in his pocket.

Rod pressed gently upon the accelerator.

The car moved forward through the village, past the houses; a few moments, and all signs of civilization fell away behind them, and there was nothing on either side but snow-covered bushes and naked trees against the blue sky.

It was a beautiful day, cold, clear, a day for skiing, a day for sleds and snowball fights and family picnics. They had had a picnic two weeks before on Jackie's birthday. Rod had gotten him a plastic disk for sliding, and another for Jay, even though his birthday was not until springtime, and they had driven up into the mountains until they had reached the spot where the snow started and there was a dip off the side of the road, just right for sliding.

They had gone, the four of them—Rod and Marian and the two little boys. Marianne had not come with them; she had said she had to study.

He could remember her face, set in stubborn lines, the softness and delicacy belied by obstinacy.

"I'm sorry, Mother. I have too much to do here at home."

She had not fooled them. She had not even meant to. She had been striking out, hurting, as she herself had been hurt. Her eyes had flicked past Rod, ignoring him, as

147

though by refusing to acknowledge his existence, she could transplant him back into that hazy limbo that his life had been before he forced his unwanted way into their family.

"I have homework to do," she had said, "and after that of course, I have to write to Daddy."

Even now Rod could feel the pain catch at his chest with the memory not so much of the neatly addressed envelopes, lying weekly on the hall table, waiting to go out in the morning mail, as of the fact that the hopeful epistles were never answered.

Marianne, he thought now, blast it all, Marianne, you crazy, stubborn, faithful-hearted little idiot!

The road had narrowed, and they were climbing steeply. Rod glanced at the mileage gauge, wishing that he had checked it when they first started. His guess was that they had come about eight miles since the village, but it was difficult to judge distance on a road so winding.

The man next to him noticed his glance, for he said, "There is still a good way to go. You turn left at the side road up there."

"At what?" Rod's eyes scanned the woods to the left, searching vainly for some form of fork.

"At the side road, up there ahead. That's the turnoff."

Then he saw it, the narrow trail leading steeply upward from the road on which they were now traveling. Rod's eyes narrowed suspiciously.

"That's not a road. It's just a hunting trail."

"You ask me the way." The man regarded him with a hint of amusement. "I tell you the way. What's the matter? You don't want to see the girl after all?"

"A car can't make that incline."

"It levels off a little," the man said, "after you get up there."

148

Rod swung the car to the left, shifted into first, and bore down hard upon the accelerator. For a moment he did not think they were going to make it. I should have chains on the car, he thought. If I hadn't been in such a hurry leaving, I could have put them on. The car lurched forward, groaning, and the tires slid and then caught, holding them suspended for an instant. Then, slowly and with infinite agony, the car settled itself to the hard pull upward.

As his companion had told him, after the initial steepness, Rod found that the road leveled off and began a steady, winding upgrade. It was apparent, also, that it had been used recently by at least one automobile, for the trail was clear of branches, and in places the older snow was marked by tire tracks. The silence of the woodland settled around them, a heavy, muffled quiet, accentuating the sense of isolation and filling Rod with a sharp awareness of the fact that there were now no villagers, no casual bypassers, no one in any direction who would hear a shot should one be fired.

Worriedly he contemplated the distance he would have to reach to grasp the pistol secreted beneath the seat and the extra time it would take to draw it out of its nesting place between the springs and bring it into action. Too long, he thought, much too long to make it even worth attempting. He would simply have to pray that having come this far, his companion would decide to take him the rest of the way to whatever end lay ahead, and that wherever their destination, Marianne would be there.

And then, suddenly, at the same instant they both saw the boy. They rounded a curve, and he was there before them, a tall, sturdy figure in a black leather jacket, limping slightly as he plodded down the center of the trail.

For a moment Rod could not believe his eyes, and then he gave a gasp of amazement.

"It's one of the Kirtland boys! The one who dates my daughter!"

The man beside him seemed equally startled. With a muttered oath he straightened in his seat.

"Stop the car!"

Before them Glenn Kirtland stood frozen, his eyes wide in shock at the sight of the automobile and the two men in it. As Rod's foot struck the brake pedal, his companion swung the right-hand door open and, half rising to a standing position, thrust his head and shoulders out above the upper rim of the doorframe.

"Hold it!" he shouted. "Hold it where you are, kid! You come here to the car, kid, and don't make funny business while you are about it!"

In the excitement of the moment his accent deepened, and turning sideways, Rod saw that his right hand was no longer in his pocket but was raised and directed at the boy on the road ahead of them. At the same instant he realized that the man's full attention was upon the boy, and without stopping to contemplate the possible result of his action, Rod made a quick and desperate lurch for the rip in the seat. Bending forward, he thrust his hand into it wrist-deep, until his fingers closed around the butt of the pistol and with a violent wrench pulled it upward, past the springs. He straightened. It had taken only seconds. The boy was still standing there. The man seemed not to have moved from his half-standing position.

With the gun in his hands, Rod hesitated for an instant. Marianne was still not with them. Until he saw Marianne, he could not afford to do anything that might leave him stranded, unable to find her.

With a second quick motion he dropped the pistol into

his oversized overcoat pocket and placed his hand back upon the wheel of the car.

For a moment he had thought that Glenn was going to bolt for cover, but the moment was past, and the boy seemed to know it. His eyes on the pistol in Juan's hand, he came, slowly and resignedly, to the car.

Looking past Juan, his gaze settled hostilely upon Rod. "What are you doing here?" he asked tersely.

"I've come to bail you out," Rod answered, fighting emotion with brusqueness. "Where is Marianne? Where did you leave her? Is she all right?"

"She's up at the cabin," Glenn's face was dark with anger. "What did you have to come for? I was away. Free, blast it! None of the others could do it, but I did! Another couple of miles, and I would have been at the village. I could have called the police from there. I'd have saved us!"

"I couldn't know," Rod said helplessly.

"You didn't have any right, coming, bringing the ransom! I didn't want anybody paying ransom to get me out of anything! I could have done it myself. Saved all of them. It would have been in the paper, all about it."

His voice was thick with bitterness. Looking at him, Rod thought, he is just a boy. He is exhausted. He doesn't realize what he is saying.

"Get into the car, son," he said gently. "I'm sorry. I could not have known. All I wanted was to get you all home safe."

"Safe!" the boy muttered. "Sure, you did. And I came all this way, twisted my ankle, practically froze to death, for nothing. Nothing."

Juan swung the car door open and stepped out, his hand secure upon the pistol. Wordlessly he motioned Glenn into the front seat and then opened the rear door and climbed in behind them.

I should have fired, Rod thought, when I could have. I should have shot him here, right here in the snow, with the gun in my hand and his attention elsewhere. Because now he is behind us, and I can't turn. As the boy says, I am fouling up everything.

"How did it happen?" Juan asked the question quietly. "How did you get away from the cabin? Are the others free also? Come, tell me. I will find out soon anyway."

"We ran," Glenn said lifelessly.

"The rest of them, they also ran? They are outside in the snow someplace?"

"The girls are back at the cabin. Dexter—I don't know. Buck shot at him."

"And the other boy—your brother?"

"He went back to the cabin." Glenn's voice was shaking with weariness and frustration. "*I* got away! I was the one, the only one! I should have been the one to rescue them!"

"It's all right, son," Rod said gently. "You tried."

The full irony of the situation was heavy upon him. Here they were on the way to the hideout, the cabin from which Glenn had fled a matter of hours before. If he had not come at all, Glenn would have completed his escape to the village and from there would have called for help without Juan's knowledge.

But what was done was done, and they were on their way to the cabin, and in a short time he would see Marianne again, for whatever help his presence could be to her.

If I only had the money, he thought helplessly. If I could only open the trunk and hand it out to them and take the children and go!

But he did have the pistol, and if necessary, he would use it. This knowledge alone was strong within him. He was a gentle man and he had never fired a pistol in his life, but with Marianne's safety at stake, he would not hesitate to do so.

Whatever was to come now, he would do what he could. Somehow he would see to it that Marianne got away and home again. He would do what he could and pray to God that it would somehow be enough.

They started slowly up the road down which Glenn had just come.

Chapter Thirteen

The cabin was quiet.

A strange quiet. A stillness of arrested motion, of things unfinished, of branches bent almost to the breaking point.

What is to come next? Marianne asked herself. What can possibly come next? For the quiet was of waiting and a final acceptance of the helplessness of their position. Whatever happened next would not be of their doing. It would come from someplace outside themselves. They could only wait.

"He is dead," Bruce had told them. "Buck is dead." He had spoken the words slowly, in an emotionless voice. "The car went off the road."

Rita had not believed him. "You are lying. Nothing can happen to Buck. What do you hope to do by saying such things, you rotten little liar?"

Was it that she did not believe, Marianne wondered, or that she would not let herself believe? Bruce had not answered. He had gone instead to the fire, and Jesse had

154

brought a blanket and put it around him and then had left the room again to return to Dexter. Bruce had sunk to the hearth, and he was there now, crouched in the same position, his eyes closed against the pain as feeling returned to his half-frozen hands. He was rubbing them slowly up and down against his trouser leg. His head bent forward, resting against his knee.

Marianne went over to him and knelt beside him. "Are you okay, Bruce? Can I do anything?"

"No." He did not raise his head.

"Do you want some soup? Coffee? Something hot?"

"No, thank you."

"How are your hands?"

"Okay, I guess. I mean, they hurt. They hurt like blazes. I guess the bad thing would be if I couldn't feel them."

"What happened to Buck's jacket?" Marianne asked him. "You were wearing it when you left."

"I gave it to Glenn." His voice was oddly blank as he spoke his brother's name. "He needed it. He was going to try to hike all the way back to the village."

"Do you think he can do it?" Marianne asked.

"I guess so. Glenn usually manages to do anything he sets out to do."

"And Buck?"

"I told you."

"But you're sure? That he is dead, I mean? Rita doesn't believe you. She is in the bedroom now with all those paperbacks of hers, reading and waiting for him to get back."

"He won't be coming back," Bruce said.

For a moment he was tempted to describe it, the blazing wreck at the foot of the cliff, the hissing sound of the orange gasoline flames as they leaped like living animals against the snow. He had drawn as close as he dared, feeling the scorching heat reaching out to him, straining to see past the blazing inferno, into whatever dark recesses lay beyond in the twisted blur of blackened metal, repeating to himself, frantically, the words that Glenn had uttered on the road above: . . . *that man was trying to kill you! That's why he went over the cliff. He was trying to kill you! . . . you don't owe him one blasted thing!*

But the words had held no meaning. Somewhere in that hell of fire there was a man. No words could make that fact less dreadful.

He had stood watching, hypnotized by horror and helplessness, until finally some innate sense of self-preservation had told him to move away before there was an explosion. It took him half an hour to climb back up the cliff, clutching with frozen and gloveless hands at rocks and bushes, wondering how he had managed to make the descent so quickly. And all the while he climbed he waited for the explosion. It never came.

When he reached the level road and turned to look down again, the flames were gone.

For a moment he struggled with the temptation to tell her, to share the experience and by so doing to make it less terrible, more like a story to be exclaimed and gasped over. But the reality was still too close to him. The words would not come.

"He won't be coming back," Bruce said, and left it at that.

He was shivering. He had been there by the fire for a long time now, but still he was shivering.

Marianne reached to straighten the blanket over his shoulders and then, impulsively, put her arms around him,

156

as she might have around Jay or Jackie, saying, as they all had said so often during the past days, "It will be all right. Everything will work out all right."

"No," Bruce said. "Nothing will ever be all right."

"But if Glenn makes it to the village, and you said yourself that you think he will, he will call for help. With Buck gone, there isn't any danger here. Rita certainly won't do anything to us. We'll just sit and wait until help comes."

Bruce shivered again, drawing a little away from her. He did not want to be touched or comforted. The ache within him was not fear; it was deeper than fear. He felt a million years old.

Glenn, he thought. Oh, Glenn, Glenn.

There were footsteps on the wooden floor behind them, and Jesse came to join them by the fire. She looked tired but oddly peaceful.

"How are your hands, Bruce? Do you think they're all right?"

"I've got some feeling back in them." He was still rubbing them up and down against his trouser leg. "What about Dexter? Do you think he's going to be okay?"

"He has lost a lot of blood, but I don't think the wound itself is too serious. We have the bleeding stopped now. He's sleeping."

Her face grew soft as she thought of the dark head against the pillow and remembered the way he had stared up at her in stunned bewilderment.

"What was that for?" he had stammered.

"I don't know." Jesse had been as startled as he was. "I—I guess I—I just felt like kissing you."

"I hope you don't make a business of going around doing that to everybody."

157

"No. Oh, no," she assured him quickly. "Actually I don't think I have ever kissed anybody in my life before. Except, of course, my parents."

He regarded her in astonishment. "Why not? A girl as pretty as you are!"

"I don't know. I guess I just never wanted to."

"But why now?"

"I don't know, I tell you."

"You're sorry for me, is that it?" His voice began to harden. "You don't have to be. If you think you're going to play the fairy princess, going around kissing cripples to turn them into—"

"What an ugly thing to say!" Jesse interrupted. "What a perfectly horrid, mean little thing to say!"

The anger in her voice startled Dexter into silence. He lay gazing up at her, amazed by the violence of her reaction.

"Just because I haven't dated a lot, because I'm not the popularity queen that Marianne is doesn't mean that I'm going to settle for any halfway kind of man, Dexter Barton! I wouldn't take a cripple on a silver platter! I'd rather go through my whole life without ever loving anybody than be stuck with somebody who wasn't fine and strong and solid! Maybe I haven't spent my life doing jitterbugs and watching movies and mooning over football players, but I have known people, fine, interesting people. I knew a Russian countess who had her land and her jewels and her money taken away from her, but she was still every inch a countess! I knew a man in Switzerland who was an amputee. He lost a leg during the war escaping from a Nazi concentration camp. And do you know, he skis! On one leg, using the poles for balance!"

Her normally pale face was flushed with emotion.

"I've heard symphonies written by blind composers and seen cathedrals designed by dying artists, and none of them was a cripple, none of them! It's bitterness that makes a person a cripple, bitterness and meanness and smallness! It's an emptiness inside them, not anything to do with their bodies!"

For a moment, when she finished, there was silence. Then Dexter said, "Whew! I guess I can consider myself told off!"

"I guess you can." Jesse dropped her eyes, embarrassed by her vehemence. "I'm sorry. I don't know what got into me. I didn't have any right to say those things."

"You sure didn't. Just like a woman, always trying to make a guy over. One kiss, and she thinks she owns him, body and soul." The words were brusque, but the dark eyes held a hint of teasing. "If the lecture is over, do you think you might, please, bandage up my shoulder?"

"Of course. I said I'm sorry."

To her surprise, she saw that he was smiling. "Say, Jesse, when you're finished . . ."

"Yes?"

"Well, you don't own a guy, body and soul, after one kiss. It's just possible, though, that after two of them . . ."

He was sleeping now. Jesse sat quietly, thinking about him, the hard, unhandsome face, the stubby lashes dark against the pale cheek. He had gone to sleep holding her hand. She liked the thought of his sleeping with his hand in hers, his face gone soft and vulnerable with all the bitterness eased out of it.

Somehow, as she sat there beside him, the tension had eased out of her as well, leaving her peaceful and unfrightened.

What will be will be, she thought now, as Marianne

had, as Bruce had. There is nothing more we can do but wait.

It was not she who first heard the approach of the car. It was Marianne who, lifting her head, said, "Listen. Isn't that a car motor?"

And even then it was a moment before the others heard it, the grinding, straining sound of an automobile mounting the last steep curve of the road to the cabin.

Chapter Fourteen

From the front bedroom Rita also heard the car engine.

She must have been sitting there listening for it, Marianne thought as the heavyset woman came hurrying into the living room.

"It is Buck!" Rita exclaimed, throwing an accusing glance at Bruce. "I knew you were lying! Nothing could happen to Buck! Now you will get yours, you lying little boy!"

From his place by the fire, Bruce did not make the effort to contradict her.

It is Glenn, he thought tiredly. He got help. We all will be going home now.

There was no particular joy in the thought. He was glad for the others. He had become fond of them during the time they had spent together. He wanted them to get home safely. For himself, however, the prospect was a painful one. The thought of seeing Glenn again, of returning with him to their home to pick up their lives as always, encumbered by his new and disillusioning knowledge of his brother's true character, was more than he could bear.

I wish I could go away, he thought. Just pack up and go somewhere far away, to boarding school perhaps or to a job of some kind, it wouldn't matter what it was as long as it was a long way off.

He was not surprised when he heard Marianne's voice exclaiming, "It's Glenn!" Of course, it was Glenn. Glenn, the conqueror, returning with the police for the dramatic rescue.

Then she added, "And Rod and . . ." Her voice changed. "Oh, no!"

"What is it?" Bruce raised his head.

"It's the other man. Juan!" Jesse had risen and gone to stand beside the girl at the window. "The one who got on the school bus with the pistol!"

"Bolt the door!" Bruce began to scramble to his feet. "Don't let them in! With four of us here, we can have control of the house as long as we keep Juan outside!"

But he was too late. Rita had already reached the door and thrown it wide and was shouting out to the approaching three, 'Where is Buck? Didn't Buck come back with you?''

They entered the cabin, scuffing snow across the rough boards of the floor.

Rod's eyes flicked quickly about the room, finding Marianne in her position before the window. Automatically he moved toward her.

"Marianne, are you all right? They haven't hurt you?"

The girl's face was blank with amazement. "What are you doing here, Rod? Did Glenn reach you? But that man? Juan. How did he—"

"Where is Buck?" Rita demanded harshly. Her voice

was beginning to take on a note of hysteria. "Why isn't he with you?"

"How should I know where Buck is?" Juan returned. "Isn't he here? This is where he is supposed to be. This was his part of the job, keeping the kids under control. Here I find this boy"—he gestured toward Glenn—"wandering down the road almost to the village! I, too, would like to know where your husband is gone!"

Glenn regarded the others defiantly. "I almost made it! I would have made it if your stepfather"—he nodded at Marianne—"hadn't decided to give in and bring the ransom. I ran into him and Juan at the bottom of the hill almost to the village."

"You brought the ransom?" Marianne asked in bewilderment. "You brought it, Rod? But how? I didn't think—"

"Of course, I brought it," Rod lied. How long, he wondered, would it be before Juan turned to him, demanding the impossible? The money. And there was no money.

He glanced quickly about, assessing the situation.

Apparently there was at the moment only one man in charge here, Juan, the one who had driven up with him. The woman must be part of it, and there was another man, this Buck, but according to the shreds of conversation between Juan and the woman, he was not here at the moment. Where was he? Coming back at any moment perhaps? Did he have a gun? Did the woman? How many firearms were there in the picture besides Juan's?

It was impossible to tell. His own pistol was heavy in his pocket. He resisted the urge to reach for it, to press his hand against the outside of his overcoat pocket, to feel through the cloth the reassuring hard shape.

"All right," Juan said slowly, "I have kept my part of the bargain. I have brought you here. You see your daughter.

She is all right. She has not been hurt. Now, I want the key. You will give it to me.''

"The key?" Rod repeated the word as though uncertain of its meaning.

"The key to the trunk. You say the money is in the trunk of your car."

Now, Rod thought, now is the time.

As casually as possible, he began to move his hand toward his overcoat pocket. I can reach in, he thought, as though for the key. He would never be able to draw the gun forth in time, but he could fire through the cloth.

This is it, he thought, and then suddenly hesitated. Juan also was moving.

"You girl," he said, "you come over here."

"You mean, me?" Jesse asked, but Juan was looking past her. With a sudden motion he reached out and caught hold of Marianne's wrist. In a second's time, while Rod stood frozen, he had pulled the girl to him and was pressing her against him. The hand that held the pistol was against her side.

"All right," he said to Rod, "no funny business now. You get the key. You take it and go out and unlock the car trunk. Then you come back in, carrying the money with you. I am going to watch you from the window. If there is anything wrong, your girl here, she is the one to get it. Not the others, but this one, this blond one."

Rod choked against the sickness rising within him. His stomach felt suddenly empty.

I can't fire, he thought. A moment ago, just one moment ago, it might have worked. I waited too long. I am always waiting too long!

Juan stood directly in front of him, in easy firing range, even through the cloth of the overcoat. Now, however,

164

Marianne was between them. Her slender body formed a delicate barrier between the gun and the man for whom the bullet would be intended.

Looking at her, at the small pale face, the soft hair, Rod felt his heart turn over at the resemblance to her mother. There was, however, a difference as well. The blue eyes were not frightened or tearful, as Marian's would have been. They blazed in anger. The girl's pretty face was twisted in revulsion.

"Let go of me!" she muttered from between clenched teeth. "Don't you dare put your hands on me, you horrid little man!"

"Oh, a spitfire we have here, yes?" Juan's voice held amusement, but he did not move his eyes from Rod. "Do not wiggle, little spitfire, or I will have to hurt you."

"Let go of me," Marianne said savagely, twisting suddenly, and then her face went white and she doubled forward with a gasp of pain.

Juan jabbed the barrel of the pistol a second time, hard into the tender area below the ribs, and the girl gasped again.

In a rage of frustration Rod clenched his fist, willing himself not to grab for the pistol. He could not fire, could not possibly pull the trigger without hitting the girl unless while she was doubled forward, he could manage to hit Juan in the head or upper chest. But not being used to a pistol, he could not count upon his aim. Encumbered by the heavy cloth of the overcoat, it would be luck if he hit the man at all. It was a risk that could not be taken.

"Stand up," Juan commanded, and Marianne did so, dragging herself painfully erect, her face now drained of all color.

"Go out to the car," Juan ordered Rod, "and get the money. Now."

"First I have to know about Buck." Rita spoke suddenly. "You say you have not seen him. Where is he? He left this morning before dawn. He was going down the mountain, looking for these boys." Her nod took in Glenn and Bruce. "This boy, the little one here, he came back this morning, later. He said the car was wrecked. I did not believe him."

"I saw no wreck," Juan said.

"The car went over the cliff," Bruce said flatly, "down where the road makes a hairpin. Glenn and I both saw it happen. It caught fire at the bottom." Watching the dawning belief coming into the woman's face, he felt a strange, inconsistent wave of pity. "I told you before."

"Is it true?" Rita demanded. Her eyes had a glassy look. She swung about to face Glenn. "Is it?"

"Yes," Glenn said. "He tried to run down my brother. The car went out of control." He paused and then added as an afterthought, "We did everything we could. We climbed down to the car to see if we could save him. By the time we got there, it was too late."

He used the plural "we" with ease. Despite his new knowledge of his brother, Bruce listened to the lie with incredulous amazement.

"Is it true?" Rita demanded again. "Is it?" She swung her gaze frantically from one to another of them, as though begging for reassurance.

"I don't know," Juan said. "It does not matter. Right now what matters is the money."

"What do you mean, it doesn't matter?" Rita exclaimed wildly. "How can you say it doesn't matter? It is the *only* thing that matters! If it is true, if Buck is dead, the money doesn't matter. Life doesn't matter! He wanted the money to buy me nice things! If there is no Buck, it doesn't matter about the nice things!''

"Be still!" Juan growled angrily. "You idiot woman, be quiet! We all knew the risks when we got into this, Buck as well as me."

"You and Buck had an agreement! Buck was to do the thinking parts; he was to make the plan, to drive the bus, to take the children! But the rest of it, that was for you to do! We were to have nothing to do with the strong-arm parts! If Buck was killed, it was while he was doing your work.'' She was out of control now, her head thrown back, her face contorted. Her voice mounted higher and higher. "If it is true—if Buck is dead—then it is your fault!''

"What do you mean, my fault?" Juan asked. "I did not send him down the mountain. If he had had sense enough to keep the children here, he would not have had to go. This was his job, and he did not do it. Only a stupid man would—''

"Don't you dare call him stupid! Don't you dare say anything about him!'' With a sudden shriek Rita threw herself across the space between them. Her heavy body struck the man from the side; her hands clawed in fury at his face. "Don't you dare, don't you dare!''

At the moment of impact, Marianne twisted away, hurling herself free as Juan's hands momentarily loosened their grip upon her. At the same instant Rod's hand leaped for his pocket.

This time he did not hesitate. With a desperation born of his other lost opportunities, he jolted the pistol into position and squeezed the trigger.

The shot was not a good one. It missed Juan completely, but the sound filled the room, freezing the occupants into immobility. Rita caught her breath, shocked back to sanity. Juan froze in an instant of motion, his own weapon raised.

It was then that Bruce moved forward.

What drove him to this action was something of which he would never be completely certain. He would have liked to have thought it was bravery, but his innate honesty would not allow this, for he believed that bravery is something that has to be contemplated. This movement was automatic, triggered by the realization within himself that someone was going to be injured. One gun had been fired, and the other was raised for action, and the stalling and arguing and hoping and plotting were now behind them. Somebody was going to get shot, somebody: Marianne or Jesse or Glenn or Mr. Donavan—and me as well, thought Bruce, me as well as anyone . . .

He was not a heavy boy, but he was wiry. There was the strength of desperation behind him as he raised his arm and brought the side of his hand down, with a sharp, slicing motion, onto Juan's wrist.

There was an instant when the pistol seemed to hang there in the air, suspended.

It was with a sense of amazement that they heard the thud as it struck the floor.

It was Glenn, of course, who reached it first and straightened to stand facing them. Tall and handsome, with the pistol held easily in his hand, he looked like the hero of an action movie.

What's it like, Dexter had asked once, *to have Superman for a brother?*

He does resemble him, Bruce thought now, with the inane reaction of restrained hysteria. With his head thrown back like that and his chest thrust out, all he needs is a cape!

"Don't move, you two!" Glenn said, addressing Juan and Rita, but Rita did not seem to hear him. With a limp, defenseless movement she lifted her hands to cover her face.

For a moment there was no sound in the room except the woman's sobbing. Then Jesse said, "I'm so sorry."

It was a peculiar thing to say, but it was Jesse.

She reached a hand out and touched the woman's shoulder. "I am sorry," she said again.

She is Jesse, Bruce thought, and Glenn is Glenn. But I—I am myself. I am Bruce Kirtland! I am, and can be, whatever I make of myself!

It was a new thought, a strange one. He clung to it now with a fierceness which was in itself new to him. I am not a shadow, a follower, I am not "Superman's little brother." I do not need to walk behind Glenn, to pick up after Glenn, to breathe with Glenn! What I am is within myself; I am *Bruce*! For what Glenn is, I am sorry, but it has nothing to do with what I am!

He stood quiet, giddy with a sense of release, as though a gigantic load had been lifted from his shoulders, a load that he had not even been aware of carrying.

Glenn said to Juan, "Raise your hands above your head." His voice was strong, masterful. He glanced sideways to see Marianne's expression, but her eyes were not upon him.

She had turned, instead, and crossed to Rod.

"Honey, are you all right?" His voice was shaken with emotion. "How badly did he hurt you?"

"I'm okay, Rod." She looked very small, standing

there in front of him. "Rod, my father—why didn't he come with you? If *you* could come, why couldn't *he*? Why didn't *he* come to get me?"

For a long moment Rod stood gazing down at her, struggling with a decision. It was the moment, he knew, to tell her, to put into words once and forever the situation which her mother had carefully concealed from her. It was time to say, "Marianne, your father didn't come because he doesn't care about you. He has never cared about you, or about your mother or your brothers, or anyone in the world except himself." It was the time, in this moment of climax—and she would believe him.

But now, standing gazing down into the small, vulnerable face, he could not say it.

Instead, he said, "We couldn't reach your father."

"You couldn't . . ."

"Your mother didn't know where to find him. She would have called if she could have. If he had known about it, your father would have come after you. Nothing would have kept him away if he had known."

"But he did know." Marianne spoke the words flatly. "I heard Buck tell Rita about it. You left messages for him everywhere. He didn't answer them. He didn't want to come."

"Honey . . ." Rod regarded her helplessly.

"He didn't care enough to come!"

Suddenly, to his astonishment, she threw herself against him, her face pressed against his chest, her shoulders shaking. The fair head, so like her mother's, was bent, her body racked with shuddering sobs.

"He just didn't care!"

Clumsily Rod stroked the bright head. "Honey," he

said awkwardly, "everybody isn't the way we wish they were. Everybody has faults. Your father . . ."

"I don't have a father." Marianne's voice was muffled against his chest. "I know it now. I have never really had a father."

Rod stood, holding her, waiting for the storm to subside.

"You have one now," he said.

Chapter Fifteen

On the way down the mountain they stopped at the village to phone their parents. Glenn stayed behind at the cabin to stand guard over Juan and Rita. And to be there, Bruce thought wryly, when the police come. Trust Glenn not to miss out on something like that!

Jesse completed her phone call and stepped out of the booth, her eyes still bright with the tears that had sprung to them at the sound of her mother's voice.

Bruce reached out and touched her arm as she passed him. "Hey, Jesse," he said softly, "did you see it? It's silver!"

"Yes, I know." She smiled at him, a joyful smile that shone through the tears like sunshine.

For a moment they stood there, smiling at each other, bound together by the simple wonder of being alive. Then Bruce stepped into the booth to call his parents, and Jesse went back to the car and to Dexter.

On the rise above them the aluminum church glowed silver in the afternoon light.

I Know What You Did Last Summer

ISBN 0-440-22844-1

The book that inspired
the blockbuster movie!

They thought the worst summer of their lives was
behind them. . . .

They make a pact: They'll never talk about it
again. And they don't—until the note. One short
sentence is enough to shatter their lives.
Someone knows what they did. And someone
wants revenge.

Killing Mr. Griffin

ISBN 0-440-94515-1

They only planned to scare their English teacher.
   They didn't mean to kill him.
   But sometimes even the best-laid plans go wrong.